# WHO DWELT BY A CHURCHYARD

*A Novel*

by BERRY FLEMING

THE PERMANENT PRESS
Sag Harbor, New York 11963

Library of Congress Number: 88-92465

International Standard Book Number: 0-932966-88-8


Manufactured in the United States of America




THE PERMANENT PRESS
Noyac Road
Sag Harbor, NY 11963

# By the Author

The Make-Believers
Lucinderella
Siesta
Colonel Effingham's Raid
The Winter Rider
To the Market Place
Country Wedding
Captain Bennett's Folly
The Bookman's Tale
The Affair at Honey Hill

*Hermione:*  Pray you sit by us,
       And tell's a tale. . . .
*Mamillius:*       A sad tale's best for winter.
*Hermione:* Let's have that, good sir. . . .
*Mamillius:*       There was a man
       Dwelt by a churchyard—. I will tell it softly,
       Yond' crickets shall not hear it.

                                        —*The Winter's Tale*

A fire between the black andirons, sinking almost to ashes then flaring up with another handful of trash—letters, records, photographs—shedding the past, the pasts. Or meaning to. Easing the load of the movers coming on Thursday ("Eight-fifteen, Mr. Embry?" "Yes. All right"), easing the load of Mr. Embry transferring his new alonenes to simpler quarters; unless he changed his mind, tried to follow the example of delighted old remarried What's-his-name who said, "She's not only a superior cook and an excellent driver, Allen, she's a registered nurse!"

In the meanwhile: Bare floors, windows without curtains, bookshelves without books like mouths without teeth. Bare walls with unfaded rectangles in the shapes of Father's paintings, now stacked in a back room waiting to be stored at the movers' (in a cubicle that I thought of as a sepulcher for his dreams).

Brown cartons about the floor boards marked for shipment to "Mrs. Ada Embry Renlap" at her new address in catchall California (divorced daughter retaining married name because of child), the very act of spelling out the shipping labels bringing back her mother's voice smiling, "If you like," to my proposal of "Ada" as our baby's name ("Ada" in my mind, no doubt, from the assonance to "Asa"—a great-uncle whose crumbling Civil War letters I had been reading, deciphering, in a search for telling bits I might use in a thesis I was writing).

And "Asa" on my mind today from the photograph I had almost burned with the rest; put aside to maybe take with me for old-time's sake (I am sentimental)—a blackened "ambrotype" of a young man looking straight back at you, hair over ears like straw spilling out of a hayrack, jacket open on a white shirt, loosely spread bow tie; young Asa, not yet in uniform, not yet writing his "Esteemed Parents" (and "Dear Miss Mamie") of "drilling, cutting paper fuses, filling cartridge bags, whittling wooden fuse plugs" at Fort Pulaski "impregnable" on the Georgia coast.

Putting it by for the moment; and stirring the fire to life with a toss of time-faded faces like words you can't be sure of, have to check out in the dictionary: A man changing a tire on a road of bare French-looking trees (surely not myself, though how else could it remind me of wiping dirty hands on a wad of emergency toilet paper my new wife handed me?); Alice herself in a beret at a sidewalk table, eyes somehow focused more on her marriage than on the husband with the Leica she had bought him; an old man, maybe 70–75, in the flat-brimmed straw hat of the day, right forearm across his cotton jacket in a leather sling (that might well have been stenciled "Chick-amauga"—Grandfather Charles, Asa's younger brother); a young woman in a floor-length skirt with a mandolin, Mother at my daughter's age; a rigid group of four, one an old lady, "Aunt Mame" by the retractable eyeglasses pinned to her shirtwaist (no kin, but "Aunt Mame" in our Southern way on account of Asa); a black man in a chauffer's cap at the crank of a museum-piece car of rods and running boards and brass canisters of fuel for the gas headlamps, spare tire by the driver's seat like a buckler ready for his elbow—all into the flames with hardly a second glance, as you don't look twice at the kittens marked for drowning.

Then fumbling behind me among the rest of

the discards and chancing on a photograph that all but spoke; all but cried, "Gently, brother; gently, pray!" in the voice of the Doctor reciting FitzGerald from his boundless memory (Frank Avrett, DMD, but "the Doctor" to most of his old friends in town).

No date on it, front or back; no description. And yet a sort of date in the picture itself, in its bringing back the summer I was night-working at the College for my long-neglected Masters (in my forties by then—incredibly!), had gone down to the coast to see again the old fort in the river that I thought I might use in my thesis on the Federal blockade of Confederate ("Rebel") ports. The date, if I bothered to look, would be the summer before the date on my M.A.—possibly two summers, allowing for some delay in getting it in shape after what happened. Anyway, close to 1962, centennial year of the bombardment.

A casual snapshot, 3x4 or close to it, black-and-white (not much color in those days); two men and a woman—an unstable setup to start with. All young; thirties, early forties. And all smiling, smiles maybe just past the peak as if I had waited an instant too long with the button: Gonzalez with his captain's bars and his clipped moustache as if he had lined it on with a charcoal stick, the Doctor with his cheerful squint I have seen on his face of forgetting the patient to attend to what he was doing to the patient's tooth, Jessica with the springing smile that I used to think of as half at her mouth and half at her eyes, watching to see if the smile was on target—had hit you—as a Civil War gunner with a spyglass might have tracked the course of a projectile (the Civil War on my mind that summer).

The Doctor and Jessica are sitting on the steps up to the porch of the Officers Quarters at the fort (not the old fort—"Asa's Fort"—in the river, a newer post below it on the bank; Spanish-American War, I think). He is a Reserve Officer (six months in Korea) ordered out for his two-weeks summer "refresher." I remember he said the orders crossed the date of his wedding anniversary and he solved the conflict, after a fashion, by bringing his wife— his new wife (two or three years "new," I've forgotten, but the Doctor, in my view, as uxorious as on his wedding day—my wife used to say he touched Jessica's hand, her wrist, as if that closed the switch on his flashlight). He doesn't take military niceties very seriously, cap on the back of his head, lieutenant's bar a little out of plumb on his collar.

His appearance and manner make quite a contrast with those of Captain Gonzalez standing at the newel post, smiling too but with a smile that reminds you of the centurion in the Bible accustomed to bidding a man come and he cometh, go and he goeth. The figure watching us from the door shadow is Sergeant Palef, detached from the Motor Pool for some sort of duty at the Quarters, not part of the picture; I hadn't noticed he was there until the film was developed (or the other figure either, at an end of the porch in a swing, a "glider," a young woman with a round Little-Red-Riding-Hood face whose name I can't remember, kin to the housekeeper, spending a few weeks with "Aunt Vertice"—and, among so many men, maybe catching one? Millicent! Millie!). Jessica's cotton skirt, pale blue, looks gray in the print. She holds her knees together as if remembering the cameraman.

An offhand photograph, coming to life in my hand as if lifted from a solution of memory-developer, filling as I studied it with the colors the camera missed, the yellow Quarters, the yellow barracks hemming the parade ground, white banisters down the porches like piano keys, the glint of brass that is the salute gun at the flagpole, the shaggy green fronds of the palm trees, the spot of red beyond the porch that is the nose of the Captain's vintage *Triumph* (he keeps an apartment in town), the corner of blue sky over the ocean, or where the ocean would be.

And with sounds, too, coming up through the years: the slapping of the palms in the persistent winds, the slapping (if you were near) of the halyards against the flagpole, bugle notes like yellow shafts of sunlight—flashes of benign lightning you could set your watch by—trivial talk back and forth among the three of them, the four of us.

And with smells. Different smells in different winds; crabs, shrimps, oysters in a land wind sweeping the tidewater flats of marsh grass and creeks with low-country names, Freeborn Creek, Turtle River, Cabbage Cut; ocean smells in a sea wind from the waves bursting open on the beach by the lighthouse (Rainbow Light, from the stripes like a barber's pole); an in-between smell in a north wind crossing the mouth of the big river, crossing the island in the channel and what was left of the great brick fort I had come to see—a dull rose-red line you could just make out from the steps on a clear day (not "Fort Pulaski" to us growing up but "Uncle Asa's Fort," from his

11

letters, hearing about them and later reading them, or some of them; hard going with the faded ink, wrinkled paper):

> . . . 2 24-pounder Blakely rifles and 8 10-inch columbiads added to our armament yesterday by the *Princess Ida* from Savannah. . . . 6 companies, 400 men at the fort. We can withstand the combined navy of the Godless Federal states. . . .

writing to his "esteemed father" by candlelight from his cartridge-box makeshift table in one of the casemates (no busybody censorship office evidently).—And eagerly,

> . . . the General has promised us a prominent position in the first engagement. . . . Our reveille is answered by 3 encampments up and down the coast, men enough, with God's continued help, to throw these Lincolnite invaders back in the sea if they attempt a landing. . . . Thanks to dear Miss Mamie for the wax tapers and candles. Thank Sister for the Christmas turkey. Howdy to the servants. . . .

(writing home a few years after the "ambrotype," Great-uncle Asa manning the Fort with his gentleman friends of the *Oglethorpe Light Infantry* and the *Liberty Independent Troop*,

12

spoiling for a chance to teach these foreigners to mind their business).—And,

> . . . digging ditches all day across the parade ground to trap the cannon balls, if they can bring their ships in close enough to fire on us, and we've got no intention to let that happen. . . . Hoisting rows of 4x12s slanting up over the powder magazine and the casemates where we live, cracks here and there you can squeeze through (if you pull in your belt). . . . Jake says there's pirate gold at the old Spanish fort on Skidaway Bluff. We'll dig it up as soon as we're done with whipping Billy Yank. . . . Ice in our canteens this morning. . . .

And other bits of his letters in my mind that put him there in the photograph—"there" as if in one of the rocking chairs lining the porch— invisible to everyone but me and my wide-angle memory-lens that seemed as telescopic as wide; out-of-focus, of course (I never knew him—unless knowing his handwriting was knowing him).

And the old War out-of-focus too; out-of-sight, long-gone, buried like the pirate gold, forgotten I thought, unless you hoped to dig it up for gain, as I did (prestige, the status of an M.A.

among my associates at the school—and in the eyes of my wife, to tell the truth). Then Gonzalez coming through with glances at the War from the other direction, changing my feelings toward him from a budding dislike to the hovering friendship you might have for a new member of your club.

Falling into talk about Fort Pulaski by the odd little incident on the beach that seemed to link the Now and the Then as my hit-or-miss snapshots did: on the hot sand one afternoon, the four of us, the barber's-pole lighthouse throwing a rod of shade across the slope like a sundial, the Doctor and Jessica wading on ahead in the sliding foam, her shoes dangling from one hand (the hand he wasn't holding), fingers in the heels, wet legs shining, Gonzalez and I standing a moment in the windy shade, divers holding back from the sun-plunge. Eyes on Jessica (or her wet legs), wading past the jetty rocks then springing back, returning to something in the sand, pulling the blue skirt tight round her out of the wet and squatting on her bare heels, the Doctor bending over to look, to scratch about the edges, say, "Crab shell, horseshoe crab," other walkers gathering to see.

Then, digging with his strong fingers as if

looping out the wadding round a patient's back tooth, "A bowling ball?" And Jessica, "It's a turtle!" everybody leaning over to look.

And Gonzalez calling, "Mortar shell," from the shade, not troubling to investigate. Then going on to me as we walked out on the damp sand when the fringe of a wave slid back, "They still wash up sometimes. Unarmed. Ten-inch, twelve-inch. Lost off a landing scow.— Leave it there, Lieutenant; I'll send some-body.—Along in here's where they came ashore, *we* did," smiling at us Rebels. "Brought in the ordnance at the siege of Pulaski in the Rebellion, pardon me, 'The War Between the States.' From New England mostly, the forces; 7th Connecticut, 8th Maine, 3rd Rhode Island. Can't say why you made the New Englanders so mad . . . ," turning away from it as you might put away snapshots of your family, re-membering the usual indifference of outsiders.

Which didn't apply to me with my thesis hanging fire, wondering if I could have stum-bled on a point of view that would round out Asa's one-sided letters. I said (to keep him talking, see if he could add anything to what I knew), "Hard to understand our people watch-ing the Federal build-up for three months without lifting a finger."

15

He said, "Four," and I said, "Yes, really four. I believe we thought the Fort was impregnable."

"No fixed position can sustain a vigorous land attack," in his centurion's voice, and a few steps farther on (as if to remind me of an instance I was overlooking), "Ten 24-pounders breached the castle wall at Badajoz in eight hours," the *US* shining on his collar. "But what could your people do? Contest the landing? With fifty-one vessels out there supporting it!" throwing out a north-south sweep of his arm at where the ships had been—and setting me to consider again the gaps in my information he might fill in for me.

I thought of telling him of Asa's jubilant (and misinformed) letter to his "Very Dear Miss Mamie" in which he said that forty vessels of the fleet had been "swallowed up among the angry billows. Can even the heathen Lincolnites fail to perceive there is a God who rides upon the whirlwind and directs the storm?" but we were leaving the beach and it seemed hardly the right time.

I was also distracted by the amusing little instant there as we turned into the dunes and the waving grasses, Gonzalez showing the way, the Doctor and Jessica following (hand-in-

hand, of course), Gonzalez—still with his "vigorous land attack"—saying, "The rifled Parrotts
made the penetration," and Jessica demurely
lowering her eyes at "penetration" then raising
them to the burned nape of his neck. Unless I
was seeing things.

Which might have been, because his "Parrotts" had already lifted me back through
many years to the parrot in a cage on the porch
of the house where the Doctor had his first
office, and his father before him, the house
then occupied by his two maiden aunts; who
loved the parrot, moved him in and out for sun
and air, ignored his squawk at any footsteps
passing on the sidewalk, "Come in! Come in
and pay the doctor!" (trained before the days of
cash on the barrelhead)—four or five of us, on
tiptoe behind the Doctor climbing to his rooms
on the top floor, fingers to lips, the aunts long
abed, Jessica Sponce (soon to be divorced—or
divorcing Sponce, I forget), Alice and I, just
back in town, maybe others now and then (not
Sponce, of course); white corn whisky and gin-
ger ale on fast-melting ice, the Doctor soon
reciting *Don John of Austria* or *Cyrano* of what-
not, and once, I remember, "Her father loved
me, oft invited me," and ending it with, "there
sits the lady, let her witness it," his muted

phonograph mixing the *Bolero* into our chatter—into the sympathetic right-left movement of Jessica's bare feet like pink puppies forseeing a romp, the Doctor starting two cigarettes and laying one between her pushed-out lips like a kiss.

And once, over his shoulder as he scrubbed his hands making ready to repair my broken tooth, "Faith is the big thing, Allen. Everything turns on faith. If I say you have a cavity in your left second molar you believe me on faith. You can get another opinion, but you still won't know first hand."

I said, "Can I have faith in that novocaine?" (which the nurse was good enough to snicker at but he ignored), going on with, "You pay me with a check and I am satisfied; I have faith in you, in your bank account. You have faith in the next man, in what he says, in his signature. If he's tricking you—or she is—everything begins to break down" (that "or she is" seeming to slip out while he wasn't looking; he going on as if to erase it), "Even if he pays you in cash you have faith in the dollar."

I said, "Used to have," but he wasn't listening, and I went on, "What about 'Come in and pay the doctor'? Your papa had too much faith, didn't he?"

"He usually got paid," smiling at his strong fingers (that he would lose one day in a moment I've never been able to explain); "smoked sausage, baskets of peaches, Christmas turkeys. That's how he got the parrot.—How'd you break your tooth?"

Gonzalez bringing me back to "now" with, "Half the mortar shells dropped off-target," over his shoulder to me, sensing I was the only one who cared, I suppose; "Paper fuses very inferior—captured from the Rebels at Port Royal." And a few sandy strides farther on, "One shell smashed a tabby wall up-river at Skidaway Bluff," Jessica laughing, "Tabby's a cat, what do you mean, 'tabby'?" the Doctor rushing in a back-up laugh like a team-mate.

But "tabby" whisking me off to the calico cat that prowled the lobby-foyer-living room of Mrs. Chisholm's *Tidewater Hotel*, where I had a room at the weekly rate—Mr. Chisholm in a baseball cap, up before day, greeting you on the porch with, "Good morning, Mister. Feeling good? Feeling hundred per cent?" greasy wind fanning his cigarette smoke landward or seaward (Rebel-ward or Yankee-ward) according to the day, drying one side of your face like a blower. "Tell Olga you want your breakfast." And one morning, "Tooth's bothering her

again. Ice cream gives her fits. Loves ice cream.
Chocolate. Dr. Ed wants to pull it. Sergeant
says no way,"—"tooth" flashing the idea
through my head of saying there was a top-
grade tooth man at the Fort, but changing it to
a noncommittal mumble that a man didn't like
to have his wife lose a tooth. To which he said,
"Wife's in Texas. With the black eye he gave
her," closing one of his own in a sort of be-
tween-us-boys wink. "Go get your breakfast.
Fried oysters this morning, if you hurry. Very
fine."

And inside, Mrs. Chisholm steering the
hotel like a helmsman, leaving the wheel now
and then to patrol the premises—the decks,
fore and aft, the companionways—with one or
the other of the daughters, not reproving, cor-
recting, nagging, just pointing. Two daughters
(Olga's age) apparently taking turns as first
mate, one husband at the filling station, one at
the hardware store but arriving on the minute
for meals at the family table by the pantry
door, everybody seeming to prefer the flow-
through of guests (of passengers) to stagnant
privacy; it seemed to me even the one-eyed
moose-head over the desk had weathered into
a benign grin, moth-eaten (more likely roach
eaten), a white piece of forgotten string dan-

gling from his muzzle. Only Olga seemed in trouble, and she disguised it.—Mrs. Chisolm said they liked to hear my typewriter, it kept them company (as if they needed it!); I said I was a history teacher, working on my notes for the fall term. . . .

History teacher? Me!—Four summers ago (five?, six?), not in a room by the week at a museum-piece lodginghouse but in a spot of somehow cosmic shade on the terrace of the *Hotel Taj Coromandel* at Madras (ordering up my dissolute third morning scotch-and-soda with a sort of Jewel-in-the-Crown smile at the lady with me—who was paying for them). How did I get here? The question switching off my thesis work as if I had stumbled over the power line to a word processor.

A wandering walk brought me to the bridge over Freeborn Creek, the sea-bound tide seeming to run it all past me on the curls and flecks of foam that made me think of Father and his rainbow "with all the beautiful colors of your life in the arc, Allen, and the two ends said to provide you with nice rewards if you can find them"; three boys with long-handled nets and baited lines scooping up surprised crabs, none of them less ready for his future than I had been: moving from fraternity house to boarding house in my junior year when things went bad at home; raking leaves in the fall, cutting grass in the spring, learning to survive on a meal-and-a-half a day (supplemented now and then after I got on the list of extra waiters at the hotel); classes in the morning, work in the afternoon, tutoring sessions for football players flunking in History, I managed to land the staff photographer's job on the college paper and ended up with enough cash to buy a new suit and attend our Commencement gala in the gymnasium—and stand on one awkward foot to be introduced to a tallish dark-haired girl from Kentucky who had been invited to the festivities by a man I hardly knew: a pre-med from home I had hardly spoken to since the dim days of Aunt Mame's school and his special high desk at a corner window ("The Doctor" not yet the doctor); had seen him here and there about the grounds, happened to take a Shakespeare class with him one term and witness the little episode in which the white-bearded professor said; " 'Her father loved me . . ,' go on, Mr., er, Mr. Frank Avrett," and turned away to gaze out at the winter Virginia trees while Frank stood and eagerly picked it up as if the professor had dropped his pencil, "'. . . oft invited me; Still questioned me . . .'" and, eyes at the cornice, continued with hardly a pause for breath to "'Wherein of antres vast and deserts idle . . ,'" the professor turning away from the window with a fanning That's-enough! gesture. "'. . . Rough quarries, rocks, and hills whose heads . . .'" "Thank you, Mr. Avrett." "'. . . touch heaven, It was my hint to speak . . .'" "Sit down, for God's sake!"

I mean we were friendly but not friends, certainly not close enough to have him concerned over my being girl-less at the festival (bank account too low to ask one even if I had had the courage, burdened with innocence and, at the moment, with the effort of trying to appear part of the gaiety). "Alice, this is Allen Embry," already starting to back away, Alice putting out a strong handshake and a strong white smile and mumbling, "O'Neal."

We hardly saw him again—now and then, stomping the white lines of the gym floor, cheek-to-cheek, knee-to-knee, thigh-to-thigh; clearly he had unloaded her. As I put it together later, Alice O'Neal was a sort of blind date he had invited on the basis of a photograph on somebody's desk, asked her for the delicious cloud of envy you stirred up in those days by bringing a pretty girl; she was pretty enough, lively brown eyes with honest eyebrows (not fussed with) and a quick noncommittal smile that he misread as promising something much more in the fast lane, and when he caught on to the truth he looked about through the pandemonium, saw me standing there alone with my forced fun-eager grin and unloaded her.

I can't begin to say what she wore but the clothes seemed somehow right, and her manner of wearing them. I had only recently acquired the word *svelte* and I was pleased to be handed what I considered an example of it. She fitted into the celebrations in every detail of appearance and manner and surface exuberance; you could hardly dance with her from one basketball line to another without being slapped on the shoulder—but most of the people who cut in didn't come back, as if they had expected a gin and tonic and found themselves with ice cream.

I couldn't understand it; I liked ice cream. But I began to wonder in our paired isolation if the details of her svelteness weren't costly decoys disguising someone even less with-it than myself (I had my A.B. but it wasn't in wordly wisdom—I hadn't even learned to smoke; I tried to fake a little savoir faire by buying a pack of the most expensive cigarettes I could find but she shook her head when I held it out to her, perhaps firming the filmy tie between us).

I brought her some champagne (New York State), which she put on the floor beside a gossamer web of right shoe—she did take a sip—but when I offered her a plate of shrimp and such things she spread a napkin on her knees and ate as if yesterday had been her last meal; I was hungry also and our two appetites seemed to hover about us as though they formed some tune we both liked to listen to. Altogether I felt very comfortable with her and said, with my mouth full of supper, that we both answered to "Al" and she nodded, was silent a moment to finish her plate then confided she had a mare at home that also answered to "Al"—gazing off at our streamers and festive decorations but really seeing, I think, her daddy's Kentucky horse farm; going on to present me with the December night when Al was "foaled," everybody tense with trying to delay the event until the stable clock got round to January, allowing her to run in the Derby as a three-year-old though actually within a blink of being four. It didn't work; she was "dropped" on December 31st and after a disappointing record Mr. O'Neal gave her to his daughter. "She has another name but she answers to 'Al' "—all of which reminded me that pretty girls can be tiresome (horses out of favor with me since the Shetland pony my grandfather gave us threw me at the age of six). And reminded me too that she came of a financial background beyond anything I knew at home even in the best days of Father's *Taylor-Embry, AIA;* it was not horses themselves that seemed rising as a hurdle in our otherwise congenial unsophistication but that horses implied money, big money, and I began to realize that most of the other aspects of this woman did too. If you had enough money you could afford to be as naive as you pleased, or as anything else; from her general unpretentiousness I figured this Alice O'Neal might well be an heiress. It wasn't fair to disparage her as uneducated, considering my own scholastic career of hopping from "C" to "C" as you might on stones across a dangerous river; she had simply majored in a different field. When she took a small toothbrush out of a name handbag and went to the Ladies, coming back in five minutes all expertly renewed and smelling faintly of flowers, I decided that she had

26

done better in her field than I had in mine; that at any rate our two levels of uneducation might well form a basis of further congeniality and I nodded inquiringly at the pandemonium on the dance floor.

We circled once or twice like a pair of pigeons trapped in the eye of a hurricane; we caught sight of Frank Avrett through the turmoil (definitely in the fast lane, with a sports number that made Alice seem like a librarian— she said, "There's What's-his-name. I think he unloaded me"). He avoided me for the rest of my stay, fundamentally a conscientious man and probably ashamed of the trick he had played on me, that wasn't a trick at all from my point of view. Or from Alice's either. When I left her at the door of the girls' dormitory (those days!) she offered me a rigid corner of her mouth to kiss and I was quite pleased. I think she was too because she said to call her the next time I was in Lexington.

We were married in the small chapel of an Episcopal church on the Daniel Boone Pike, nobody happy about it but us two, Mrs. O'Neal in tears, friends (a handful) sympathetic, Brother Denis definitely hostile and Sister Mary disgusted, Mr. O'Neal as unpleasant as if I had managed to trade him out of a Derby three-year-old. They saw me as a fortune-hunter, gold-digger, and of course they were partly right, but not in the cold, calculating way they had in mind. I loved this unassuming forthright rich girl (money no fault of hers), hadn't been able to get her out of my head during the six or seven years of my search for a job that agreed with me: to the Head of the History Department with A.B. in damp hand, suggesting a monitor's job in one of his several sections ("Come back in ten years" the substance of his answer); to a cut-rate motel that took me on as night clerk and extra bartender (disguising the truth with "assistant manager" for my trusting parents). When I later found something on the late shift of the morning paper the midnight hours seemed to combine with my pay of $27.50 a week and start a change in my patronizing attitude to money; after all, it wasn't anything to hold against a dear friend.

We had written; I had called her on the phone now and then, managed to appear in her town two or three times: pleasant meetings for both of us I thought, though quite unbelievable by modern standards, a little food, a little beer, a little easy laughing, a little holding of hands, a little kissing—handicapped by the

primitive state of contraceptives in those days
but stumbling through.

And stumbling through my ignorant jeers at
money as I circled in closer to it and lost some
of my queasiness about it in a way that reminded me of fishing-days with Father and
learning how to unhook a catfish without
being finned; I couldn't help picturing the delightful things she and I could buy that neither
of us was enjoying on his own. Not that she
was deprived of any specific thing; Mrs.
O'Neal promoted her (both the sisters) in
every possible social way, supplied her (them)
with plenty of activity in the world of horses,
tennis, swimming, cocktails and all that, but
nothing seemed to take hold; golf, possibly, at
which she was very good. I met her once in St.
Louis, watched her win something rather big
and we both got rather drunk and forgot our
longstanding antediluvian inhibitions, or
some of them.

Four or five years in Europe, I've forgotten.
Paris, Geneva, Oslo, etc., etc.; springs at An-
necy, summers at Etretat (where I broke a back
tooth on a piece of oystershell at "Madame
Oitre's" shellfish counter by the Casino), win-
ters looking on the Mediterranean—it was like
riding a surfboard on Pacific rollers (or the

29

pictures). She paid for everything, of course; or funneled the money through my empty pockets so I could pay, watched over my money level as you watch the level of gas in your tank, fill it up from time to time—with high-test. She had a delayed sort of Irish humor and we laughed a lot, laughed about her visit to the Swiss gynecologist when she thought she was pregnant (hoped, I think; she wasn't), about my going to the chirugien-dentiste with my tooth and changing my mind in his waiting room and fleeing; other women didn't interest me any more than a field of VWs would have tempted Father and his *356 Porsche.*

But sometimes I had bad days; my bringing-up seemed to follow me like a persistent dog. I said one morning at a sidewalk cafe over a third ten-o'clock bloody mary, "If I had to make a living I'd starve to death." She said, "Is your tooth bothering you, lamb?" I said, No, I was thinking about the man my Presbyterian father used to tell us about who buried his money in the ground so he wouldn't lose it. She said, "You're getting tired of Oslo, honey. We'll go on a cruise."

We had been on cruises in the right seasons—North, South, East (not West)—but it was the six-weeks cruise to the Indian Ocean that she then bought for us which finally led to my background's overtaking me; not so much the cruise as the price she paid for it: $17,185.43 "not including gratuities to the ship's personnel" (to quote the glossy four-color prospectus). It bothered me all the way to Madras and the *Hotel Taj Coromandel*, where I paid for our British scotches (with her money) and said, "Honey-Alice, baby, I've got to go home.—And it's not my tooth, it's something more complicated." She said, More complicated than a tooth?, and I said, "If I had to make a living—"

She said we had been through all that, was silent for a minute, looking at me the way a doctor looks at the blood-pressure gauge, then said, "What's the matter, honey?" in the voice of a mother saying, Where does it hurt? She dismissed my trying to explain that I needed to measure myself against the breadwinners of the world: "That's just hypochondria, love. You wouldn't like bread if you could win it."

I said, "Nevertheless," and she thought for a minute then reached for our traveler's checks ("our"!) and said, "All right, lamb. Go pay our bill."—We held sweaty hands all the way to the sweaty airport, quite a distance.

31

*Berry Fleming*

When Frank Avrett was repairing my tooth he
stopped humming long enough to tell a nurse
who interrupted him from the door, "Say I'll
call him back," and in a few minutes from
behind my head as he scrubbed his hands,
"Board meeting. We're short a history teacher"
(referring, I assumed, to a private school
founded while I was in Europe's playpen—he
was on the Board of Governors). At the front
desk as I was reaching for my check book
(mind on "Come-in-and-pay-the-doctor") he
said over my shoulder, "Weren't you into History at our blessed college?"

I got the job, nepotism of a sort though it
was—American History, first-grade English,
elementary French, study-hour overseer, a sort
of academic handy man; not, I suspect, just the
sort of faculty member they had in mind but
adequate (they hoped) for getting them
through the rest of the year. They nodded as if
gratified when they heard I was taking night
classes at the College for an M.A. in History
and hired me for another term.

Alice couldn't understand any of it. Misun-
derstood, took it that the beauty of her finances
was fading, losing its appeal for me, and that it
was time to shift into another gear: if she was
going to have a baby she had better get on with
it. (We had talked about adoption, a boy,

32

someone to carry on the Embry name, but it didn't appeal to us—too chancey; your own could be chancey enough.)

She felt about a Lexington doctor much the way I did about Frank Avrett and she went home to check things out with him (and be with Sister Mary through the court ordeal of her contested divorce—the family could easily bear up under my absence), and I drove down to Mrs. Chisholm's *Tidewater Hotel*, circled next day over to Fort Screven on the riverbank and was surprised to find my old friends on the front steps of the Officers Quarters.

But what surprised me more, when I left them to drive about the Post, was the sight of the young woman who had served me my "fried oysters this morning, very fine"; she was arm-in-arm with Sergeant Palef on a palm-bordered sidewalk near the hospital—I didn't know Palef's name at the time but I remembered his face.

"Lieutenant," from the Doctor's nurse in his door at the hospital, "there's a sergeant at the desk wants you to look at his wife's tooth," the Doctor telling us bits of it in an offhand manner a few days later in the shade of the porch—Gonzalez, Jessica, Mille and me ("Aunt Vertice" ignoring us, pacing the porch like a deck officer, keys jingling at her waist belt). He had fitted her in, not very busy; saved the tooth. Removed the nerves from three root canals, capped the tooth with something or other, I don't remember his clinical terminology; a two-hour "procedure." No problem. No charge. "Good patient. Gave her some medication for when the anesthetic would wear off—"

"Palef's wife?" from Gonzalez.

"That's what he said."

"His wife's in Texas, supposed to be. Short black hair?", the Doctor saying he hadn't noticed, didn't think so, was thinking about the tooth, Gonzalez already unbuttoning a pocket of his shirt and starting to scribble something in a brown notebook.

And Sergeant Palef disappeared from the Officers Quarters; he had had some sort of snap assignment there but it didn't survive the reprimand to his commanding officer. The next time I caught sight of him he was in charge of a detail of prisoners in brown fatigues with carts and brooms and buckets of black paint sweeping and freshening up the flagpole area and the little pyramids of cannonballs ornamenting the salute gun; his three stripes were intact, but the reprimand was on his record, no help in advancing his rank; he looked sullen, snapping at a man in a voice like a whip to clean up a spot of paint spilled on the walkway (and making me think he wished his prisoner had been Captain Gonzalez—or the tattletale Doctor Lieutenant).

I am weak on military chains-of-command, but I take it that Gonzalez, who was on the Colonel's staff at headquaters (adjutant or something) reported Palef through channels for disciplinary action: trying to pass off his girlfriend as his wife to get free treatment at the hospital.

As adjutant he seemed well posted on Palef's marital troubles a few months back, telling us with a detached smile of Palef's fistfight with the "other man"—a Corporal Somebody—and what looked like a real possibility "somebody would end up shooting somebody. Brooding sort of chap, vindictive. But, after all, you don't like somebody else getting in your bed." Jessica said, Maybe she invited him (with her sidelong smile), and Gonzalez said, "Even so." He said he managed to have the corporal transferred to Texas; "Fort Bliss. Where Mrs. Sergeant, I understand, soon joined him—black eye and all."

Palef himself waiting for the Fort bus at the

35

stop near the hotel—ironed and creased, hands behind him, feet apart, eyes on something (or nothing) across the street, not thumbing a ride, not asking anything, quite able to manage; a picture, I thought, of the professional soldier. I stopped the car and he ran a few yards and tumbled in, with a silent nod as if to the bus driver (a civilian).

For myself I was already back to the few words about him with my landlady the afternoon before: on the beach, the tide in the stage a dozen fishermen seemed to fancy, some on the dripping rocks of the jetty, some on the sand casting into the surf, reeling in, casting again, all of it stitched together by lighthouse shadow on the sliding water. A figure in hip boots in the surf up to his knees (her knees), reeling in from a cast into the waves and shouting over the water-sounds, "Catching your dinner, Mr., Mr.—," turning back to her pole.

Then wading out on the sand at the chance of a moment's talk, not sure of my name but associating me with the Fort and "Vertice and little Millie"; asking after them and turning away in a minute with, "Sweet little thing but she'll never get a strike. You've got to fish with live bait, Mr., Mr.—"

"Al Embry, Mrs. Chisholm."

"—Mr. Al. Olga knows. May hook the Sergeant yet—God help her!" laughing a little,
doing something to her line and adding, "Sergeant's a game fish, Mr. Al. Barracuda. Mean.
Men get mean once you give it to them," with
a laugh that set her coughing. . . .

Mean or not, he was mostly silent on our
drive to the fort; responding to a few words
from me now and then, but negligently, in
monosyllables (reaching me in faint puffs of
chewing tobacco, not offensive), as if he didn't
recognize me, though he must have seen me
taking the snapshot of Gonzalez and the others
on the steps. For a while I thought his silence
indicated nothing more than the distance he
felt between soldier and civilian, but by the
time I let him off at the gate I was wondering if
he didn't cast me in with Gonzalez and the
reprimand, and was allowing some of his resentment to spill over on to me—as it might
also spread out on to the Doctor-Lieutenant,
given the spreading quality of resentment, the
viscosity.


All of them standing in the round umbrella-
shade of the palm trees near the dock on the
river as if taking shelter from the downpour of

midmorning sunlight, Jessica, Millie, the Doctor, Gonzalez; standing aside while a detachment of trainees from the summer school thudded past on their hard heels singing with a mandatory gusto and drummed on to the platform ferry.

Millie's wave as I passed was invitation enough. I put off my visit to the great fort ("Asa's Fort"), parked the *Chevy* by a flowering crape myrtle (the *Triumph* had the only shade) and joined them. "They're firing the big gun!" Millie said, as pleased as if promised a ride on a merry-go-round, pulling some pinches off a ball of cotton and handing them to me. "Save your ears," as we followed Gonzalez on to the flat deck and the pilothouse on the upstream rail. I told Jessica she and Millie must feel like a pair of salmon trying to swim against the current, with all the young stares streaming into their faces. She said, "Faces?" with her laugh, squaring her shoulders an inch or two.

And on across the river to a sunny seacoast BATTERY CLEVELAND, the letters in white on the black concrete, the name itself giving it away as of a younger generation than BATTERY LINCOLN and BATTERY GRANT on the mainland that had fired on Asa and his Fort Pulaski even if Gonzalez hadn't flung an offhand, "Spanish-American War" over his shoulder, leading the way.

And in a minute adding, "Twelve-inch disappearing rifle," in the voice of a chef mentioning herbs he knew his diners weren't up to appreciating. "Obsolete with air reconnaissance but handy for training," and as we passed, calling over the Lieutenant to be introduced (who touched his cap with a minimum of enthusiasm and hurried away to check in person "the level of oil in my recoil cylinders").

None of it of any use to me and my thesis; different wars, different guns—and yet the same eagerness to handle them as in Asa's time, leaving me interested in a subsidiary way. More interested than the others, I thought; certainly than the Doctor, who seemed to be wondering why he had come, attentive though he was at giving the ladies a hand on the high steps up to the gun level and again up to the command post and its view of the sea beyond and the great prurient gunshape below—now in the midst of young trainees stripped to the waist springing this way and that in a run-through of the loading drill, two ready with the ramrod, two with the projectile dolly at the elevator from the magazine like a dumb-waiter from the kitchen up to the banquet room; two with the stiff canvas cover off the breach, folding it and stashing it away "just so" behind a corner (flashing me an ironic memory of the "trainees" in my classes lolling in their freedom to listen to me or dream).

Gonzalez handing his binoculars to Jessica beside him at the window, pointing at the tugboat on the sky line and the brown square sail of the target half a mile in tow, Jessica briefly searching the view as if trying on a hat that wasn't her style then offering the glasses to the Doctor at her other side—who shook his head. Millie rested young elbows for a moment on the hot concrete and glanced through them with a remote smile for the tugboat, passing them on to me as the Lieutenant appeared on the steps from the gun platform, spoke a few professional words to Gonzalez and dropped out of sight.

"Bad news, everybody," in the centurion voice, translating. "No firing this morning." A chain on the lift from the magazine; maybe two hours before they could raise a projectile.

Millie's the only disappointment I could see; a quick glance about showed the rest of us looking at each other as if testing for support in what we didn't quite like to say: Two hours! In this heat, this glare! This black concrete stove!

This frying pan! (vaguely discourteous to the U.S. Army, which had tried)—our reticence translated to action by the opportune *honk* on the ferry's electric horn, and the Doctor's making a move toward the steps, the wharf.

A wasted morning for me, it seemed at the time; only one brief moment with any meaning beyond the obvious, and I wonder if I am not reading more into that one than was there— the moment growing out of the great phallic gun lying there at rest in its cradle as the gun crew went into the drill for a simulated fire, rolling the dolly in and out from the lift (empty), heaving the breechblock closed with a musical Chinese "Gong!", fastening the hook of the lanyard cord; gunners hopping to posts and stock-still as pieces in a half-done chess game, eyes on the Lieutenant's teeth as if watching a mouse-hole, a tension in the whole enclosure like the short quiet in a lightning storm, the Lieutenant raising an arm at "In battery," and bringing it down at "Trip!"—and the gun lifting in an even almost eager arc and thrusting forward as the head of it cleared the lip of the rampart. And Jessica watching, entranced, giving an audible gasp and clutching Gonzalez by his bare brown forearm.

At the ferry rail the Doctor, silent, stood

between them, Millie and I on the Captain's other side. Gonzalez said, "Pulaski," with a wave upstream at the rose-brown flick on the yellow river like a chip of pinewood, the name bringing me back to my reason for being at the Coast like Aunt Mame's school-bell after recess.

"Asa's Fort," with "8 10-inch columbiads added to our armament yesterday by the *Princess Ida,* fired on all the way, a most gallant exploit" (and his quoting the Bible to reassure his girlfriend at home, "They shall fight against thee, saith the Lord, but they shall not prevail, for I am with thee, to deliver thee").—Aunt Mame, for me an ancient lady in the door of her school with a handbell so heavy it snapped her elbow straight to ring it; in her seventies by then and following the line of print in your first-grade reader with a yellow pencil as long as your six-year-old forearm, pulling your eye on in jerks just ahead of your voice as if to lift you up the next riser of a steep stairway.

Five in the school, maybe six, counting me and Frank Avrett, "Miss Mamie" to some, "Aunt Mame" to me—black umbrella-skirt to the bare floor, blunt black shoes peeping out like mice, a single white hair curling from a brown spot on her chin. A bare room off the upstairs back porch of a nephew's house where she lived (tolerated, I suspect, but maybe not), low tables, sawed-off chairs, bare windows like gentlemen in shirtsleeves, black coal scuttle by the stove on a metal pad that caught your shoe, roll-down map on the wall of The Confederate States of America.

"Miss Mame" to my father, pulling up a peg on the brass cribbage score board (glancing up with a wink at her reaction through his pince-nez); "Aunt Mame" to my mother, half her age but inviting her over for occasional afternoon "tea" with an aroma I couldn't identify though the tall bottle it came from was by a leg of the teatable. And when she had gone (pinned on her hat with a pearl-topped foot-long skewer and gone), " 'Aunt Mame'? Where's 'Uncle Mame'?" "Aunt Mame never married, honey." "Why? Wouldn't nobody take her?" " 'Anybody.' Now you run ask Harold if supper's nearly ready."

And Aunt Mame, on Memorial Day (Confederate), invited to the Monument Street porch to see the parade: the *Oglethorpe Light Infantry*, the *Richmond Hussars*, the *Liberty Independent Troop* (new editions), and still newer editions of "the Academy Boys" in gray-top kepis, blue jackets, white pants ironed to a saber's edge, all in step (more or less) behind the Shriner's Band, wheeling past the Monument (to the three Georgia signers of the Declaration of Independence) into Greene and on to the ceremonies at Magnolia Cemetery—the Civil War veterans behind like a baggage train, some on foot with sticks, some in surreys.

"Grampa," to Asa's younger brother, "why ain't you in the parade?" " 'Aren't,' " from my mother crossing Grampa's, "Takes me back to—"

"But, Captain Charles," from Aunt Mame, "you were in more battles than any of them— Shiloh, Gettysburg, Chickamauga—and your arm still giving you trouble." "Pants won't button any more, Miss Mamie." "I could move the buttons for you, Captain."

"Takes me back to one time when I . . ." and going on, usually, to tell about the other parade; not Memorial Day, "Independence Day," 1869, the view of the Monument guiding him to it like a lighthouse beacon: arm in a leather sling, fingers stiff as pencils from a Chickamauga "miniball" in the forearm, civilian jacket a little tight after his three years in the open air, hurrying down Monument Street

44

through the crowds, trying to get home before
the parade, new wife alone with the baby—
"With *you*, Daughter"—the town full of hood-
lums, riffraff, freed slaves, black soldiers of the
*33rd Ohio*. "Evenin', Cap'n Charles!" hands in
his pockets to show he didn't need to touch his
hat any more. "You better come on back to
work, Luke. We're shorthanded at the store."
"No, sir! I'm thoo with work, Cap'n Charles.
I'm a free man now." "What you going to do
for a living, Luke?" "Do, Cap'n? I'm going to
enjoy my freedom—"

A roll of drums from up the street breaking
into a blast of band music that shocked the
black crowd like a cattleprod; they flooded past
him to the curb, into the road.

" '*We are coming, Father Abra'am, three hundred
thousand more . . .*' "

(reciting the words in a way that brought you
back the tune also). Hurrying on, picking his
way, trying not to touch any part of them, the
crowd opening once to let through a handful
of young blacks in fantasticals, bumping and
pushing their wild way, faces streaked with
colored chalks, one in a torn frock coat and a
stovepipe hat, the bare black feet all round him

45

breaking into an irrepressible jig as the tune, coming closer, banged into a sudden new cadence:

*Bring the good old bugle, boys, we'll sing another song . . .*

He could see the lightfooted horses at the head of the column and the dancing shine of the brass horns in the sun. There would be flags in the black ranks behind all that; flags of the *33rd*, but flags of the Union too. To be saluted? Hat off with a left hand? (thanks to one of their miniballs in his right)—
"Out of the road, old Rebel!" from a black sentry in front of Haskell's Saddlery Shop, waving at him with his long bayonet, he escaping into the street under the nostrils of a leading horse—"US" everywhere: "US" branded on the sleek haunch of the Colonel's horse, "US" on the saddle blankets, "US" on the collar of the mounted black bugler, bugle at his hip. "Out of the way, Rebel!" "Hold on now, I've got to get home to my family." "You'll get home in the lockup you ain't mindful!" hustling him back into the smells.

*Sing it as we used to sing, it, fifty thousand strong . . .*

The first platoon wheeling into Monument
Street in a front that stretched across the road,
rocking with the band, caps cocked over black
ears, white gloves in line on rifle butts, white
gloves swinging on the long big-handed
arms.—He gave up. Couldn't escape.

"Wheeling past the monument, Peter, to
Georgia's signers of the Declaration of Independence."

"Yes sir, Captain, we know the Signers
Monument."

"American Independence, Peter! Not Southern Independence. They didn't sign Confederate Independence—"

"But, Captain Charles," from Aunt Mame,
"you wouldn't want our country split in two
pieces."

"Miss Mamie, they split in two the greatest
union of civilized people the world has ever
known," (mixing his advocacies, but he was
getting old—and had already forgotten what I
wanted to know): "But, Grampa, did you take
off your hat?"—the 1910 blare of the Shriner's
Band blowing away his answer; Captain
Charles, Asa's younger brother.


To the great fort on the island one day ("Asa's
Fort"), four of us and the reinstated (partly

47

reinstated) Palef from the Motor Pool to manage the outboard—a little withdrawn in manner perhaps but unfailingly "correct." The Doctor couldn't come, or said he couldn't; involved with physicals on a new busload of trainees. And cool to the idea of Jessica coming without him: "Do you really want to go? It'll be a furnace," overlooking the possibility she was getting fed up with army-post life on her wedding anniversary.

"It's all right, Frank!" a little annoyed at disapproval. "Millie's going. Allen too. Maybe Mrs. Housekeeper (what's her name?). It's safe, for God's sake!"

"Gonzalez?"

"But of course. It's his idea. Or Allen's. Those Civil War bugs." (I putting it back together from mumbled bits between her and Millie in the boat—Aunt Vertice disdaining the whole expedition.)

Up an arm of the river that was almost still as it met the tide like the flat hand of a traffic cop, joined its red-mud color with the pale sea water to make a color like the salmon-colored brick you use for inside walls protected from the weather; paler than the brick of the Fort that were meant to withstand not only wind and rain but the storm of siege guns (the Par-

rotts) of any enemy misguided enough to attack.

"BATTERY LINCOLN in there," from
Gonzalez, waving at the shore. "Behind the
dunes. You can't see it. The Rebs couldn't find
what to shoot at."

"'Confederates,' please!" from Jessica in
make-believe indignation, Gonzalez laughing,
"Yes, of course," and going on to point to-
wards, "BATTERY GRANT, along in there.
And SIGEL a little farther up with the Parrotts
that made the penetration"—while I pressed
the camera button at what views I could see
(and wondered if there weren't realities "behind the dunes" I couldn't see, behind the
camouflaging banter); and behind Palef's sideways look at the Captain?—hand on the tiller,
facing up the channel as if listening only to the
motor sounds, but eyes pulled round to squint
at his reprimand and the source of it? Maybe
not.

Hardly any current, the rose-brick walls of
the Fort rising out of the band of marsh grass,
the great pink split of the penetration opening
as we passed; continued on round the island to
the channel side and the dock (or a replacement) where the *Princess Ida* "added 8 10-inch
columbiads" to Asa's armament—Millie

49

springing ashore past my overage offer of a hand.

A salute for the Captain from the caretaker, shifting his stick to free his right hand, Gonzalez acknowledging it with an easy, "Good morning, Sergeant" (and a respectful glance at the wound stripe). "My friends would like to look round your fort, if that's convenient—"

"Yes sir, help yourself, sir," pointing up the white-sand path with the stick, in his right hand now.

Heels on the wooden bridge over the moat like an amateur drum corps, frogs in expert dives into the thick green water, Stars-and-Stripes flopping on a pole above the entrance in a tempered land wind, and a view through a tunnel in the walls like sighting through a pistol barrel, or the barrel of one of Asa's muzzle-loading muskets—except for the sunny red spots at the end, that became ripe tomatoes strung up on stakes in a military line on the parade ground. And behind them a row of low green cabbage plants like a rear rank, and off beyond, two white-trunk sycamore trees like volunteers in a forgotten war; nothing left of Asa's "ditches across the parade ground to trap the cannon balls" before they hop-skipped into the powder magazine, or his "4-by-12s slanting up over the casemates," the casemates all open in a border of rose-colored arches that reminded you of the cloister of a monastery.

I was taken back to Asa's "flowing well" when Gonzalez asked the caretaker what he did for water, the man hopping about on his damaged leg to point with his stick at the gushing pipe by the entrance tunnel. "Fine water, sir," with a wave at the overflow draining away into the moat through a grating of castiron letters that had been chipped to make the "U" of USA into a possible "C"—the only momento I could find of Asa's gentlemen friends of the *Oglethorpe Light Infantry.*

A tall woman obviously dressed from the Quartermaster's shelves—caretaker of the caretaker, it seemed—held out a kitchen cup of water from the pipe which Jessica accepted then handed back at a sniff of the low-country sulphur smell, Gonzalez mumbling, "Little sulphur won't hurt you," grinning with his big even teeth and leading the way off through the weeds to the great triangular gap in the casemates and the mound of shattered brick beneath the "penetration"—led me back to his "Parrotts" that had made it; and further back for an instant through the mound of years to "Come in! Come in and pay the doctor!", Jessica on a threadbare sofa chattering to my wife in a sisterly mumble too quiet to conflict with the Doctor's *Don John of Austria,* or his "Rude am I in my speech and little blest . . .," or what not—or once his juggling with the text to make it say, "That I have ta'en away that young man's lady, it is most true; true that on that very sofa she promised last night to marry me," leaning over to kiss her and touch the bracelet on her left wrist he had given her.

Gonzalez and I ("those Civil War bugs") up an iron stairway to the ramparts and the wind like a furnace blast, the ladies below in the sycamore shade with Mrs. Caretaker as expansive hostess. "BATTERY SIGEL somewhere in there with the Parrotts," waving at the south bank; "you can't see it for the dunes," leading the way on round the abandoned—surrendered—ramparts, the sea wind moving from one ear to the other as we reached an angle, nothing left but concrete flats on the sand to ease the ghostly heaves of young gunners aiming ghostly gun-carriages.

And ghostly bits of Asa hovering over me like gnats: "A fine sight to watch one of our cannonballs flying through the air, striking the water and bouncing up to strike again, the way we used to make stones skip at Avrett's Pond" (in a letter to "My dear Miss Mamie"). And in one to his "esteemed parents" that first January, "Nothing along the beach to break the wind and we slept on the sand wrapped in our blankets, everybody trying to get on the leeside of somebody else. In the night" (turning his paper sideways to scribble bottom-to-top) "the tide came in and caught us. Cut holes in a cotton sack for my head and arms and had a dry shirt—until the Lieutenant came by."

And in one to "Esteemed Father: The Billies are up to something on the south bank, we can't see what. And on the north bank too. Major says go take a look, who'll volunteer? Who wouldn't! Everybody volunteers. Corporal Haskell points at me (you know his uncle—has a saddlery shop in Monument Street). Tomorow night. Blackface like a minstrel show."

. . . up the river, paddling close to the bank where the current was slowed by the tide coming in—the north bank—the marsh grass in a wall higher than their heads; off the channel into Flybird Creek and then another turn into Mud River and a head wind from the sea that blew in new sounds over the sawgrass that stopped them as if they had run aground,

Haskell giving a hiss like a cat and digging a paddle in the bank, the two of them rigid in the boat trying to read the sounds coming through like shapes obscured in fog. No wind-borne words, no voices, yet voices of a sort in the ponderous sound of unseen objects groaning, grumbling, protesting, all of it rising and falling in the wind gusts.

Motionless in the boat, hardly breathing, waiting for an answer as you wait for a strike on your line or an overflight of ducks; then Haskell, losing patience, pulling up his paddle and pushing on to a bend in the creek—and a translation of the puzzle into a view of foggy shadows moving in the yellow light of windy flares and beyond them what seemed to be two flats in line towed by oarsmen in rowboats, each flat low in the water under the shadow of what looked like a siege howitzer or a columbiad, too long for a mortar. Black shadows of Billies moving by signal and mutter and muffled whistle, some on the flats, some ashore on what must have been a firm landing place (or what they hoped was firm), heaving long planks for a runway from the flats to the shore, and while he watched through the reeds and blowing grass, heaving a gun carriage on to the planks (or trying to) and sinking knee-deep in the mud, one wheel of the carriage sliding off the runway with a wind-blown crunch into the marsh and a wind-blown burst of Yankee cursing that brought a jubilant wave from Haskell in the bow—and a whining bullet past their ears out of the tall grass, from ahead or behind or beside they couldn't guess.

And didn't stay to try to, plunging into the January water on the side away from where the ball came from (or might have come from), mouth full of half-swallowed fishy water, hoping the side of the batteau covered the top of his head, kepi floating off on the flooding tide that was lifting them minute by minute out of the grass screen.

Silence for a space except for the wind scratching the sawgrass with a sound of sandpapering a board, then a sound of plunging strides into the mud, into the high grass, then silence again except for the water-sounds against the batteau, the tide-sounds, pulling his mind off the rifleman (who might have stopped to reload) to the current flowing in that would carry them on to the Yanks and the landing place—and a Yankee prison pen, if not a Yankee rope. The same thought striking Haskell as if carried by the sides of the boat they both clung to and feeling the boat being pushed back toward the river they had come in by.

Pushing against the spongy creek bottom when he could reach it, swimming when he couldn't, thinking of the sentry and his re-primed musket, of the mud and the sawgrass that (God willing) would hold him and his

55

cussing. . . . "The Major thanked us, but he wasn't very hearty. Said back up off his rug, we were dripping puddles on it—"

Gonzalez, at a corner of the ramparts, looking over at the wharf we had come in by, "What's he up to?" just an exclamation and mostly under his breath, pointing at down-there Palef in the boat with a wrench in his hand and the motor laid over the stern. "Never mind. Good mechanic—if tricky soldier."

Leaving it to face again the great five-sided cloister (that Asa, dutiful son, had written home about), pointing at a corner in line with the penetration: "When the Rebels saw the Parrotts had the range of the magazine . . ." and finishing his "when" with a turning up of both his hands; leading the way to an iron stair and down among the blowing weeds and across to the ladies stirring in the shade like a trio of disturbed bees. Millie greeting us with, "She's lost her bracelet!" in the monotone meant for fatalities. "When did you have it, honey?" Mrs. Caretaker turning Jessica's wrist in her fingers as if to make sure it was gone, and Jessica staring off ahead as though for an answer to When did she have it?, Gonzalez saying, "The penetration threatened the magazine and—lost your bracelet?"

Jessica deciding she hadn't. "I didn't wear it. I'm sure. Almost sure." She had it on her dresser, planning to wear it—he liked to have her wear it, had given it to her as an engagement present—then she remembered he wasn't coming. She had left it in the room, was sure, afraid of losing it, a little too large; Gonzalez taking her wrist and looking at the size of it, front and back, then pressing her hand in a message of Don't worry, it'll turn up.

Which none of us, I think, expected it to do if it had fallen off among the shards and shattered brick the Parrotts had scattered about the penetration, though we searched among the chips along the base of the mound, up and down the slope of broken bricks, Gonzalez offering a hand to the ladies (which Mrs. Caretaker spurned, insulted).

Then back through the weeds to the regimented cabbages and tomato vines, and Sergeant Caretaker pushing himself up from a cowhide chair with his stick.

"We may have lost a lady's bracelet," Gonzalez to him in the centurion voice. "If you find it send it to me at Headquarters. Captain Gonzalez."

But that wasn't the way things developed (the Doctor telling me later—at the restaurant party, I think): Sergeant Palef appearing at the hospital desk, bowing to the nurse with the same movement as taking off his cap and asking if Sergeant Palef might speak with the Lieutenant.

The Doctor said, "Tell them to sit down," assuming the visit had something to do with the root-canals procedure and a little annoyed at the prospect of needing to cope with imaginary female dissatisfactions. The nurse said he was alone, and the Doctor grumbled, "Show him in," continuing with his signing a printed form in triplicate and looking up to say, "Good morning, Sergeant" at the sound of heels on the office linoleum.

Palef said with some starchiness (recalling to the Doctor an instant's memory of the reprimand, the disciplinary action), "Sir, I understand the Lieutenant's lady has lost a piece of jewelry," the Doctor nodding, eyes on the sergeant's brown fingers unbuttoning the left pocket of his shirt and fingering out the bracelet.

"Where did you find it!" more exclamation than question, unimportant where he found it, it was found, mind already léaping to what sort of reward would be right for such a service; money from a Reserve Lieutenant to a professional soldier? Irregular perhaps, but—

"One of the men found it, sir. I believe he was cleaning the Captain's car,—sir."

"Captain Gonzalez? Found it near the Captain's car?"—quite possible, though; the car usually parked by the porch near their own; they were passing it constantly. And did it matter where the bracelet was found? It was found.

"*In* the car, I believe, sir."

Surprising him, as when you find you have omitted something and your bill may come to more than you bargained for. And yet it added up to nothing, was really quite reasonable; they had all been in and out of the car, Gonzalez showing it off, talking "tachs" and "sticks" and "revs," grinning like a new father (foster father, the car clearly "adopted"). "Who found it, Sergeant? I'd like to thank him. Give him something."

The sergeant wasn't sure. The man who found it left it with the chef at the Officers Mess to pass on to the housekeeper, who knew all the ladies; the cook showed it to Palef and Palef said he knew who the owner was, was going near the hospital, would return it direct to the Lieutenant.

"Well, thank you very much, Sergeant. And

thank the others for me," which the sergeant acknowledged with a miniature bow and heels smartly together (as replacement, I suspect, for saluting a reserve medic lieutenant).—And left my old friend standing at his yellow GI desk gazing at the bracelet in his fingers as if trying to read the *Jessica Avrett* and date inside the band, which of course he couldn't do in that light—or trying to stare down uneasy thoughts before they formed.

And seeing them form in spite of him, shape themselves into a pre-construction of the moment when he would be handing her the bracelet: "It was found in Gonzalez's car," watching her eyes. "Impossible! Who says so?" "Palef says so, Sergeant Palef." "I lost it at the Fort, Frank; or on the way," eyes sparking. "Palef said—" "He's mad with Hamilton, Frank. The reprimand and all that. It's on his record, can affect his promotion—" " 'Hamilton'?" "Oh, 'Captain Gonzalez,' then." "You haven't been out with Gonzalez?" "What do you take me for!" (not quite denying it?) . . .

Grateful to the nurse for her rubber-soled entrance with more blank lines for *F. Avrett, Lt., CAC Res.*, receiving them with a thank-you that was hardly audible and the inaudible paraphrase to himself, "She deceiv'd her husband,

and may thee," like the jeer of street kids at a passing cripple.—(And maybe more he didn't tell me.)

At the Saturday parade ("review," "march-past"—whatever they call it), in the shade with Jessica-and-bracelet, Millie and "Aunt Vertice"; talk among them about the bracelet, which I hardly heard (found in the boat when the orderly was cleaning up . . . Sergeant Palef told Frank it was found in the Captain's car . . . absurd . . . anything to involve the Captain, you remember their run-in . . . miffed at Frank too, for giving him away . . .); I wasn't listening, thinking of the little soldier-civilian display I was seeing: Gonzalez playing his part of adjutant with the neat minimal precision of a finalist at Forest Hills, saluting the Colonel eye-to-eye, wrist right, elbow right, all moves with a somehow clipped edginess; and Doctor Frank at the end of the front away from the band with his half-dozen from the hospital like a spare tire over a rear bumper, moving to the center with the company commanders but moving with a sort of civilian walk, a round-edged moving, in step with the beat of the music but walking, not marching.

The difference hardly noticeable in the

march-past itself—in "the heavy lightness of those that are marching, many together"—the ground dry and sloughed into a gray dust by the time the Doctor passed (offering the Colonel a sort of friendly greeting with one of the pale hands that had saved Olga's tooth—and my own, indeed), all of us standing as the colors passed, my straw hat at my left chest but my mind back with Grandfather Charles and the colors of the *33rd Ohio* about to pass him at the Monument: "But Grampa, did you take off your hat?"; the blare of the Shriner's Band blowing away his answer (if he made one), his son-in-law Peter, my father, at the head of the *Oglethorpes* (new edition) with a stride somewhere between amateur and professional—between the Doctor's and the Captain's, the flags stretching out up-river in the sea wind. And Aunt Vertice tilting her ashen head to whisper in my ear, "Millie's birthday today," as if the band was celebrating it, the whole parade.

She was having the chef do a birthday cake; "With sixteen candles. Sensitive about getting old. She'll be twenty-one, but don't tell," raising what was left of eyebrows at me for my understanding. I must come; Millie liked me (the Southernism, meaning nothing); six o'clock; some fruit punch on the porch, then

moving into the dining room and some music
on the phonograph. Of course I was "delighted."

But I think both of us were glad when
Gonzalez, hearing about it, came up with
something more festive, fitting birthday into
wedding anniversary, which Jessica must have
told him of.

Into the city for a birthday-anniversary party at
a place he knew of; Jessica and the Doctor with
him three-abreast in the *Triumph*,; Millie and I
in the 90,000-mile *Chevy* (more room for the
Doctor with us but he declined) everybody
polished for the occasion—shaved brushed,
shadowed, tinted—but Gonzalez putting the
gentlemen to shame with his starched whites
and the glint of his brass buttons (the Doctor in
fresh khaki with Korea ribbon—the best he
could manage as amateur soldier); *Chevy* following *Triumph* into town and to his rooms for
preliminary champagne—not much talk in the
*Chevy*, what with the years it would have had
to cross: "Sixteen! I'll never see twenty again!"
when I teased her with what Aunt Vertice had
said. I said, even so, there were compensa-
tions, and she looked at me as if searching for

the ones I had found, then dismissed me, leaping on to, "Marriage? No thank you. I have a married sister," with a half-laugh. She didn't know what she wanted (as who does, I thought, until you get something like it with some of the parts missing)—the door of the Gonzalez's apartment opened from the inside as he fumbled for keys by an astonished young woman with well-kept shoulder-length hair of a color not matching the chocolate-red *Triumph* but harmonizing with it. I thought she handled her surprise with considerable know-how, firing blank smiles at each of us then firing a second one at Jessica that somehow seemed loaded. "Kris," she said, as Gonzalez stumbled over names (himself surprised); "With a 'K,'" which seemed to fit with her general Scandinavianness.

The Doctor seemed quiet at our table for six but I might have seemed so too, the band-boys so carried away with their drums and cymbals and brasses you thought twice before convincing yourself your words were worth the battle; an attitude apparently confined to us (older than the rest, or most), no shortage of exuberance elsewhere. We danced with the birthday-girl and the friend, and of course with Jessica, danced in our out-of-date, out-of-place, thrifty, walking-the-plank way—Kris taken out of my arms almost immediately by friends of other evenings (one of them a man of Gonzalez's age with a beard trimmed like a trowel about whom she mumbled as he approached, "Oh, here's a man I used to sleep with").

She didn't introduce him—maybe didn't remember his name—but I think of him as "Domino One," the domino that started the tumble in the old analogy of "falling like dominoes": his dancing with Kris annoyed Gonzalez (perhaps his manner of dancing, or Kris's responsiveness) who, intending to annoy Kris, danced repeatedly with Jessica, which annoyed my old friend the Doctor (watching them with little darts of his eyes, on the dance floor and talking side by side at the table), disguising his annoyance—or meaning to, I thought—with a skimming account of Palef's returning the bracelet, as if reminded of it by the bracelet itself on Jessica's wrist glinting at the other end of the table as though consorting with the glint of the Captain's insignia. "Said it was found in Gonzalez's car. Mistaken. Not at all, of course. I looked into it; naturally. Found in the boat after your trip to the Fort—no matter," adding a fill-in question of How were things with me at the School? but turning his eyes to Jessica and Gonzalez on the dance floor now, not to me for an answer.

I answered anyway; said I liked the School, they hadn't complained of me, not to my face anyhow, even seemed pleased at my doing night work at the College. "I'm doing my thesis on the Blockade, I told you that. Down here looking for I hardly know what—centennial of the siege, you remember; the surrender." I was adding good-naturedly, "Another anniversary," as he touched my wrist with an apologetic "Excuse me, Allen" and walked away maneuvering among the dancers to claim Jessica from the Captain as you might reach for a piece of your air luggage that another traveler seemed on the point of mistaking for his own.

Leaving me there at the table, amused that the anniversaries should be including Millie's birthday but led on into memories I had of him—always seeming baffled at why I fretted about getting an M.A., fretted about having a job, with money in the bank (even if it was my wife's money, or her old man's). He had "money in the bank" too; top professional standing, lived well, summer house at the Lake, sailboat, motorboat. But as I see it, I don't think he realized that, after his wife, the most valuable part of his feeling of well-being was his practice, his profession and the world of medicine; without that I thought he would be as disconsolate as I had been that morning on the terrace at Madras. He didn't see it that way. He was looking forward to retiring, to "selling out"; planned to travel, of course, visit those faraway places he had heard about (Madras probably). Come home to hammocks under trees, no doubt; cold glasses of this and that, children bringing the glasses, probably; but certainly a pretty wife to love him, and to love (in that order).—And taking no chances with this last detail by lifting her arm (and bracelet) from the Captain's shoulder and laying it, them, on his own, Jessica accepting the change-over as you do a fade-out of the sun.

Kris sitting down, eyes on her friend down the table as he gave his hand to astonished Millie, lifted her out into the churning noise as if for a dive into the surf; Kris smiling at them as though she had told him to do it, give the little kitten a treat, a swim with the lifeguard himself—tossed him Millie like a trainer tossing the fishlet to the eager porpoise; the "fishlet" delighted in this case and bouncing to her feet at his wave at the dance floor.

"Protégé of yours?" over her shoulder to me,

patronizing my overage presence. "Or of Gonzalez, maybe? His favorite age" (and Mr. Domino's "favorite age" too, it seemed to me, accepting his assignment with some of the eagerness of the propoise).

I summed up briefly who she was, watching her through the crashing breakers of the drummerboy and his cymbals, admiring the way she adapted innocence to experience, covered it with an old-time feminine wish to please, with responsive smiles over teeth the Doctor had probably already noted with satisfaction; ending my watching with a nod of "Excuse me" to Kris and claiming Millie for my out-of-date steps—to which she adapted as neatly as she had to Mr. Domino's.

And adapted her talk too: "Your grandad was at the big fort?" to put me at ease with something I could converse about.

I said, "Great-uncle," but the instant it flashed me of Asa faded quickly to the college gym and talking with my Alice at the Graduation Prom, thinking they were of about the same age (and innocence), and conscious of a sort of rainbow-arc affection for both of them; not as tall as Alice, to my nose instead of eyebrows, and more of an armful. Light on her feet in a way you could feel in your fingers.

And Half your age!, the thought so loud in my head she might have heard it, only three inches from her ear.

I wondered, more secretly, if there wasn't some place without drums and cymbals we could talk (my designs on her of an antique innocence—as far as I could tell), talk about herself, of course, but I was willing to listen; perhaps she would listen to my traveler's tales of years she hadn't visited. I had been pleased that Alice offered me a corner of her mouth to kiss—

"I won't be riding back with you."

"What did you say! This racket—"

"I said—"

"Never mind. Why not?"

This pair of interlopers had asked her to go on with them to "another spot" they knew of.

I mumbled something unenthusiastic, which she dismissed with a move of thin shoulders. I thought "great-uncle" was about the category she put me in and I wondered if great-uncle gave me the status to show I disapproved; when I wouldn't care to diagram why, if she asked. I couldn't say I didn't like what I thought this knowing duo might be planning to introduce her to; it wasn't up to me to protect her.—And maybe it was time for Little Red

Riding Hood to meet some denizens of the Dark Forest.

"Tell Aunt Vertice not to worry," as if sending a message ahead to Grandmother. "They'll bring me back."

I was saying, "But don't you think—" when Domino returned, dismissed me with a nod and took her away, leaving "great-uncle" with his miniature jealousy to thread his way back to his half-empty glass on the table.

Thinking "jealousies-in-the-air" and trying to escape them (or one of them) in Great-uncle Asa's mission with Corporal Haskell on their other expedition,

" . . . inviting me to come in about the voice you invite an enlisted man to 'Fall-in!' What worries the Major is some sort of activity on the riverbank below the Fort his spyglass can't explain. 'Paddle over the back channel to Jim Island. Here,' jabbing the wall chart with his finger. 'Yes'r,' from us. 'Make your way down the riverbank to the beach, they may be bringing in stuff from the fleet. Guide on the lighthouse.' 'Yes'r.' 'There are monkeys on Jim Island. They'll run from you. The snakes won't.' 'Yes'r.' 'And neither will the Yanks.' 'Yes'r' (the only way to answer a Major)."

Drizzling rain when they pulled the batteau out of the water (half out), slid the flat bottom over the greasy mud. You could just see Tybee Light through the tops of the grass blinking like a left-behind lightning bug, two miles off or close to it; no monkeys or any sign of them, no sound except the wind rattling the sawgrass and the clucking of the current under the boat. And the sound of Haskell, after a look all round like the turning Light, scraping through the reeds like a swimmer with the breast stroke, Asa following close (good-soldier, but also not to be left alone in the wet blackness—not quite pitch, he could see his hand if he held it against the sky); Haskell stopping after a few steps—a few breast strokes—and raising his arm in a halt sign, a listen sign as if pointing at the new sound that seemed so out-of-place in the marsh, in the dark, he couldn't account for it. The measured pounding of a carpenter's hammer was what it sounded like (and couldn't be), distant and faint but there; five or six bangs, quiet, five or six bangs.

But the riddle answering itself when they crawled to the edge of the marsh, pushed shoulders out of the sawgrass like rats out of a haystack: pale sand in front of their noses slanting up into dunes right and left along the riverbank in what seemed a continuous natural dike following the river (and baffling Major's spyglass on the ramparts of the Fort). And along the near side of the barrier a good imitation of a nest of hornets (of yellow-jackets—in the yellow lantern light, the hooded flares); clearing, leveling, pounding, laying out pine logs and crossing them with a flooring of planks until there was no question they were building a gun emplacement, and probably for siege mortars, from the cupped shape and the height of the side toward the Fort—no guns, no armament; not yet. Making ready.

And making ready with splinter shelters for the gun crews, shelters for arming the projectiles; and farther down a make-do road that looked as if it had almost made itself under the wheels of the lumber wagons, a larger shelter halfway to another beehive of activity as though servicing both, Haskell pointing and mumbling, "Surgery," then nodding down-river toward the lightning-bug lighthouse, and setting out again on their elbow-belly-kneecap slither through the tough stalks of the marsh grass—on and on, with elbows wearing out, and knees, and CSA belt-buckle scooping up cold sand by the pantsful.

And passing other swarms of "jackets" building other nests, digging, flooring, driving pine-smelling posts into the sand, crossing them with timber, sandbags, mud, weeds from the marsh and he couldn't be sure what; more "jackets" already than the Fort's whole garrison. But no cannons? Mumbling to Haskell, resting a minute on worn-through elbows, worn-through knees, "Got no cannons. No big guns," and Haskell mumbling,

"Guns or no, these folks mean business," crawling on like crocodiles.

And coming at last to the lighthouse and the beach—and to his questions wrapped in answers: mortars, columbiads, James rifles, Parrott rifles, kegs of powder, slings of shells, all being lowered from five vessels offshore in the half-light into lighters with decking built across the gunwales and towed into the ebbing surf by rowboats. On his belly watching it, hardly breathing, all but nauseated, thrown back to the boy watching a coming storm from the hayloft window, lightning with thunder on the tail of it like a game of pop-the-whip, rain hiding the house like a sheet of canvas, and in a moment the bolt of lightning and the smell of burning hay, all of it seeming to follow an ordered sequence beyond his experience, controlled from somewhere beyond his influence—shaking off the dream-storm for the storm building up in front of him: a lighter into the shore on the rise of a wave, careened by a rope from the beach until the gun rolled off, forty Yanks (fifty?, a hundred?) dragging it in above high-water line—Yanking it in.

Something inexorable about it, storm-like, tide-like, not to be diverted; literally breath-taking—as he stared at them in the bad light, in the surf-sounds, the slicing sounds of command whistles as men and shadows lashed a pair of skids to the axel of a sling-cart, one end of the skids, then dragged the gun by cables to the midpoint, rolled another sling-cart over the slanted ends and (at a whistle with a sawgrass edge) raised the. . . .

Gonzalez dodging through the tangled exuberance—the tangled (to my ears) music—and dropping onto a vacant chair beside me with, "Don't you love 'em! They play you on until you bite and then they gaff you," tossing it off with a flip of the wrist.

I supposed he was thinking of Kris as the "gaffer" (with her undisguised welcome of Mr. Domino), but Jessica and the Doctor appeared in the tangle like insects trapped in spider-web music and I wondered if his gaffer might be Jessica—a quick wonder, gone in a second, put behind me by his finishing something he was saying with, "Enjoyed it all. Be sorry to go."

I said, " 'Go'?" and he said, "Monday, first thing. Washington with the Colonel."

I said I was sorry to hear it, had hoped he might arrange for me to see the old Federal gun emplacements along the riverbank (restricted for some reason, "off limits"). He gave no sign of hearing me—I thought he didn't, with all the turmoil—gazing off at the band or the dancers, or particular dancers; possibly Kris and the man with the trowel beard she

74

"used to sleep with," possibly Jessica and the Doctor, because his, "Beautiful dancer" certainly applied to the feathery moves of Jessica's feet and legs (and certainly did not to the Doctor's dragging shoes, going where they should but tardily, without much conviction).

He said, back to thinking of his trip, "Colonels rate an entourage, you know. A hand for the briefcase." Then in another leap that baffled me for a second, "Tomorrow afternoon?"

Of course I said, "Fine," as soon as I made the connection; I had been at the coast almost a week, had seen the Fort again, seen the surrender (through the eyes of eighteen-year-old Asa), taken some pictures, repolished my general feel of the shore, of the winds and waves that hadn't changed since Asa's day—in short, had gathered up enough "extras" to spoil my thesis and would have to discard them. If I could see the old gun emplacements tomorrow I would go home early Monday and start pulling it all together—before I began falling in love with Little Red Riding Hood (not to replace my Alice but, like the Walrus, "to give a hand to each").

We divided the bill, the gentlemen calculating "thirds" in low asides as though exchang-

ing lubricities (in olden times), the ladies turning away to talk among themselves as if to
allow us privacy in zipping up our pants.

I was saying, again, "Don't you think—" to
Millie, when Kris took her arm and steered her
away waving thanks for the evening.

The Doctor mumbled at my ear, "All right if
we ride back with you, Jessie and me?", and
we ended our anniversary-birthday-(coming-
of-age?) party with waves to Gonzalez and a
girl in the *Triumph* and the three of us folding
ourselves into the front seat of the *Chevy*—
rather quietly, I thought; and the quiet continuing. I did mention to the Doctor the trip to
the old gun emplacements tomorrow, the only
time Gonzalez could manage it, and he said
with I thought a noticeable satisfaction, "Yes,
off to Washington, Monday, he says," Jessica
turning her head to the car window in a way I
read as annoyed, though I wasn't conscious of
anything to provoke her and dismissed it as
part of the usual unwinding of festivities.

I said, "Tomorrow afternoon," and went on
to invite them ("with Millie and the Captain if
you see them") to the porch of my offbeat hotel
for cold drinks when we returned. "You
mustn't go home without a visit to the *Tide-*

*water Hotel,"* the Doctor nodding without enthusiasm and Jessica not declining.

But it didn't work out that way.—I spent Sunday morning typing up my notes (the hotel
quiet, with everyone ironed and creased and
hatted and walking off to church, Mr.
Chisholm lagging like a dinghy on a ten-foot
tether), decided about noon I couldn't face
Mrs. Chisholm's Sunday dinner and got a
sandwich at The Greek's; the empty phone
booth by the girlie magazines suggested I
might well firm up our schedule, rather casual
as I remembered it, and I called the Officers
Quarters.

Aunt Vertice didn't understand, had never
heard of "Allen Embry."

"Who? Hold on.—Talk to this man, Millie,
Embers Somebody."

"Hello? Hello, Allen," as present through
her voice as if she stood there, had skipped
unscratched through the tangles of the Dark
Forest, I mumbling something like, "Well! You
got home?" that sounded like Mama asking
What time did you get in?

She said, "I got home," as if smiling—half

smiling; holding back? (none of your business?).

I said something foolish like How was Mr. Domino? (fishing for some details like a jealous adolescent), to which she responded quickly with, "Can't talk now, Allen. Jessie just had a telegram. We're in a tizzy. Wait! Here she is—Jessie!"

And Jessica seeming quite upset: a telegram from her brother-in-law phone-delivered from Savannah; her sister was in the hospital, car accident, needed her; no details. She had tried to call the man but couldn't reach him. She would have to go, but if she took the car it stranded "Frank", he had another week. I thought of offering to drive her home, but she clearly wanted to leave right away and I didn't want to miss our trip to the old emplacements—and I confess, the prospect of a three-hour drive with Jessica didn't appeal to me (any longer, I might say—rather uncomfortable nowadays, in my back-number way, at the feeling she gave me much like wading in a stream subject to unexpected changes in depth). I said if she took their car I'd bring the Doctor back with me, I could use a few more days at the coast.

She seemed quite upset; said she didn't

know what to do until she could reach the brother-in-law. Anyway, she wouldn't be going with us to see "those damn things up the river." And we left it at that, not my concern—I hadn't even known she had a sister—and nothing to go into over the phone anyhow.

All resolved by the time I got to the post: their car gone—leaving a space between the others like the gap after the Doctor makes an extraction—the Doctor himself sitting in the front seat of a sheenless spotless Jeep talking to Sergeant Palef beside the fender with a rag, or listening to him, half-listening. I heard Palef say something like, "Madam has left us, sir?", which the Doctor answered with a sort of what's-it-to-you grunt that held, I thought, a lingering edginess at "madam's" not being there.

"And the Captain leaving tomorrow," (innocently?—not linking the two absences?—just showing awareness of our little get-togethers, unusual enough to be noted in the kitchen?).

The Doctor grumbled, "I believe so," turning to me with, "Hop in, Allen," as if to brush away his own awareness of the pair of absences, hardly turning his head as Gonzalez skipped down the steps in rough shoes and fatigues, buttoning the cuffs of a fresh shirt to

79

make long sleeves; "Mosquitoes," with a little
laugh, interrupting the buttoning to acknowl-
edge the sergeant's salute and adding a,
"Stand down, Sergeant," in the centurion
voice. Palef's Very-good-sir seemed almost in-
subordinate in its over-correctness, but it was
hardly audible as he leaned over to make a
quick swipe round the grip of the steering
wheel, moving on to insert himself in the other
back seat beside me (bringing along his faint
sweet smell of chewing tobacco I had noticed
on his other ride with me), Gonzalez continuing in a casual tone, "Brought along a little
artillery," as he laid a holster-and-pistol on the
floor by the gear shift and whipped aboard
with some of the agility of his dancing;
"Monkeys no problem but you wake up a cottonmouth now and then. All right back there?"
to me as I worked to fit in my feet and knees—
lifted by his "cottonmouth" back a hundred
years to Asa and Haskell crawling through the
sawgrass,

.... bellies-elbows-kneecaps, halfway back
to the creek and the batteau, Asa so hypno-
tized by what he had seen of the Yanks and
the hauling in of the guns he had forgotten to
count, hesitating when Haskell asked how
many mortars he had seen, how many colum-

biads, then saying, "Eleven, all told," not to be caught out.

Haskell saying, "Eleven nothing! Close to twenty—Christ a'mighty!" with a jerk of his head, and, "What the hell!" and, "Son of a bitch!" springing out of the grass and trying in the dark to get hold of his knife to lance the bite; which he couldn't do, one hand going dead from the bite in the upper arm and maybe a second bite in the side of his neck, Asa beside him in the nearly-dark trying to find the bite (bites?) for some vague plan of sucking as you sucked an orange, squeezing it like a sponge—

The whole moment suddenly taken out of their hands as the Yanks alerted: shouts from a working detail, four or five of the nearest throwing down shovels, picks, hammers, pouncing on muskets from a stack until it seemed like half the battery was on them, hurling them into the mud, Asa gasping, "Snakes!" through a mouthful of cold dirt; "Snake got him!". Causing a sort of throwback change in them from soldiers to what they were before soldiers, mumbles back and forth among them, suspicious, then curious, then compliant, holding a lantern to find the bite (bites?), and "Get the Doc!" from one of them in a cold-country twang with stripes behind it; "Get him to the surgery, you, Saugus!"—ignoring Asa as if he had been an empty powder bag—two of them running away, Haskell stumbling along between them half prisoner, half patient, the other Yanks trailing with Haskell's musket and his haversack and hat, Asa plunging waist-deep into the marsh grass as the Yankee voice yelled, "Grab the other one!"—dodging through the tangled weeds that gripped his legs like fingers, tripping, sprawling into the mud, wriggling on as if the dark was a cave to hide in if the cottonmouths were willing. . . . "My love to dear Mother, and to yourself, Father. Howdy to the servants. . . ."

Gonzalez braking to a stop at a chainlink gate blocking both ruts of the road and dangling some keys on a metal disk over his shoulder toward the sergeant. I thought the Doctor in the front seat might offer to take them and open the gate (we two packed in the back tight enough for shipment) but he seemed hardly with us, gazing ahead at the gate and the sand road; he might have been looking beyond at the first of the old emplacements but it was all but indistinguishable under the blown sand of so many years, the waist-high weeds waving in the hot wind.

Blown sand against the bottom rail of the gate, Palef dragging it open only far enough to let the car squeeze through and dragging it closed again, saying nothing (or nothing audible) to Gonzalez's, "Latch it, don't lock it. Leave the keys," and following on foot the short drive to what Gonzalez introduced as, "BATTERY STANTON, range close to two miles. Screened by the dunes," with a backhanded wave at them. " 'You-all' couldn't spot it from the Fort," smiling at one of us then the other to be sure we appreciated the "you-all"— hard to tell if the Doctor did or didn't, eyes on the sand road that was hardly more than a trail, two gray tracks separated by knee-high grass that scraped with a watery sound against the bottom of the car.

"Splinter shelter," (as we climbed out on to the sand), nodding toward a black cave in the slope of a dune, a rotted log over the entrance for a lintel, the wood eaten away except a few slivers of bark. "Popular with the local lovebirds until Colonel ordered up the fence. That larger one" (with a wave of his wrist) "probably the Surgery, midway between two batteries to service both—," voice fading out for me in the memory of Haskell and his snakebite and the Yankee voice shouting, "Get him to the surgery!"

The "surgery" (I suppose) bringing me round again to the Doctor—silent and hardly turning his head to see what Gonzalez pointed at, the three of us aboard again and bouncing among the shallow washouts in the trail, gripping whatever knob or rail or handle we could lay fist on. And I wondering why he had bothered to come with us at all; then answering the question for myself (or partly answering it) as I remembered that his Jessica had gone home, leaving him possibly with an empty Sunday afternoon and the flat deserted feeling we husbands sometimes get of having a pillow pulled from under our heads.

Which led me on into Palef's offhand coupling of his "Madam has left us, sir?" with "And the Captain leaving tomorrow," not meaning (most likely) to suggest a connection between the two events except that it changed the makeup of our little group (which he was on the fringe of through the incident of Olga's tooth and the run-in with the Captain); though of course I didn't know what he meant, nothing or much—his point of view as far from mine as his quid of tobacco from my cigarettes—walking on ahead of our bouncing low-speed car and the Captain's "BATTERY LINCOLN," "BATTERY SIGEL," as we passed; ahead of my back-thinking to our party and the dancers, Domino with Millie, the Captain in his summer whites-and-brass-buttons with Jessica, the Doctor and I at the table watching—watching, I thought, through our large and small jealousies.

Adding that to what I overheard Palef saying to him (in all innocence, perhaps—or perhaps not, given his breach with the Captain?), turned me to another guess as to what might be behind my friend's remoteness. Could he be questioning Jessica's reason for leaving, doubting the story of the sister's accident, or thinking it exaggerated? No confirmation of the story; no phone-delivered telegram to read until the mail came, tomorrow at the earliest. And with doubts spawning doubts, as they did, was his imagination leaping over probabilities and seeing her, not at her sister's bedside but with Gonzalez in Washington?

I thought the chances were that mine was the imagination doing the leaping—there among the sand ridges and time-bitten shelters and magazines and antique gun-emplacements that I was fast losing interest in, fast accepting that these old relics had no place in the thesis I was working on. Probably no such doubt of his young wife had occurred to him; and if it had, all he needed to settle it was a phone call to the sister's husband, his own brother-in-law, showing a reasonable concern about the sister's mishap—or even just posting him that Jessica had left, would be there later in the day.

Gonzalez stopping the car at a tumble-down emplacement that he called Battery Something-or-other, gesturing at five imaginary "thirty-pounder rifled Parrotts, siege carriage. We can see the Fort from the top of the dune," reaching back to gather up the holster from the floor and hooking the web belt over his fatigues, the four of us then pushing up the soft slope and from the crest getting a clear view of the rose-brick walls and the great vaginal opening of the Parrott's penetration—Asa's Fort.

And for me (seeing the pistol and the Fort) a sudden return of Asa's scribbled lines about a pistol that a friend of his "was handling with a heavy glove, the day very cold, when the hammer escaped from his fingers, the bullet shattering the bones of his ankle and foot. . . ." Which brought back another scribble about "a bullet penetrated Leroy's haversack and stopped in a loaf of stale bread he was saving for his supper. . . ."

About to mention these ancient echoes, when Gonzalez lifted his left hand for quiet, eased the pistol free of the holster and fired it

with a shocking blast at something among the
rotted planks of the gun platform, growled out
a "Damn!" and fired again, the snake whip-
ping away into a space between the planks.
"Up too late last night!" (as if to say it before we
did), returning the pistol to the holster but not
hooking the fastener as though thinking of
other targets.

Then turning away to our view of the Fort
with a summary of the end, "Sent a man with a
flag at sunrise April ten, Lieutenant Somebody, I've forgotten, Connecticut man. Back in
an hour with a note from the Rebel in command: 'It is my duty as it is my inclination to
defend this Post to the last extremity' "—smiling at the non-Yankee bombast of Asa's Colonel.

And throwing me back to Asa's cheery letter
of three days before:

" . . . everything goes well with us. We are
prepared to make a formidable and successful
resistance—4 8-inch columbiads in the casemates and 3 42-pounder guns; 10 10-inch columbiads on barbette, 3 12-pounder brass
howitzers. . . . A few nights ago on sentry,
just at sunup, saw a black dot right in front of
my head. God said to me, 'Move your head a
little bit, Asa, that's a bullet!' and it whizzed

by my left ear. If He hadn't warned me I
would have seen the ball that killed me. . . .
Picture me now on a bed of clean pine straw
with a blanket and you have my luxurious
sleeping arrangements. . . . The convoy of
provision steamboats to the Fort by Com-
modore Tattnall was a most gallant act, fired
on from Mud River and Flybird Creek. . . .
The Sovereign Disposer of all events has given
them over to blindness and madness and is
leaving them alone to contrive their own destruction. We are ready to fire at them 25 shots
an hour—if we can locate their batteries
cleverly concealed behind piles of sand and
sea grass. . . . Warmest love, my dear parents. April greetings to Miss Mamie. . . ."

All of us plowing through the "piles of sand
and sea grass," through veils of gnats and mosquitoes contemptuous of the wind, Gonzalez
ahead (host of a sort), the Doctor a few sandy
yards behind him, Palef off to one side on the
landward slope as if underscoring his non-
commissioned status—or still in a huff from
his collision with the Captain? (The idea pulling after it a tangle of thoughts I was hardly
conscious of until later looking back: one of us
disgruntled, one sulky and maybe jealous, one
absorbed in his pointing at this and that,—and
one loaded service pistol; brushing it all away

with a fanning swipe at the mosquitoes.) And a by-the-way mention to Gonzalez that there seemed to have been no censorship scissors in those days, that I had seen a letter home from a young soldier saying the Fort had provisions for seven months. "Handy information for the Yanks, I'd say. Named the garrison: the *Oglethorpes*, a company of Irish troops, a company from West Virginia 'under Lieutenant McIver'."

Not troubling to reply for half-a-dozen soft strides along the top of the dune then turning to say almost the same words he had used last week on the beach: "No fixed position can withstand a vigorous land attack," going on to wave down the slope at the ruins of "BATTERY SHERMAN, three 13-inch seacoast mortars, iron bed . . ." and some other talk about it that I didn't hear for going off at a tangent and placing his "fixed position" and "attack" in a context they weren't intended for, giving them other meanings as we children used to do making cloud shapes into animals and faces—that changed as you looked. Reading his "fixed position," for an instant, as Jessica? And his "attack" as maneuvers of Gonzalez? All of it vanishing like the cloud animals in a wind.

And yet leaving me with enough "cloud animals" in mind to make me glance again at the Doctor's bent shoulders ahead of me and wonder if some such fleeting imaginary pairing of the two might be what was troubling him, contributing to his quiet, his apparent indifference to our little expedition, hardly turning his head at, "BATTERY SCOTT, iron carriage, front pintle . . ."

A wondering, farfetched or not, that led me off into half-questions, shuffling through a deck of them as, years later, I would be glancing at the old photographs before spinning them into the fire—half-questions, dim as Asa's ambrotype; such as, Had he really been annoyed at watching them dancing at the party, watching her gay responsiveness to a non-husband that I thought was as instinctive to her as touching her ears with a scent she enjoyed (and thought the non-husband would too)? And of course he had many other parcels of memory to see her through that I didn't have—though I did remember the months of their intimacy (maybe years?) before her divorce, and I did wonder if he was saying to himself something like his old recitation in our college classroom, "She has deceiv'd her father and may thee." Wondered if he was seeing such half-formed doubts as growing into the larger one created by her and Gonzalez now chancing to be absent at the same time—or not "chancing."

On along the ridge of the dunes, the flattened crest, Gonzalez, the Doctor a few strides behind him, then myself (Palef below on the slope), Gonzalez saying into the wind something about many of the projectiles turning end-over-end, "Half-scraped grooves, probably—farm-hand cannoneers. But white flag after twelve hours." On a few steps, then, "Casualties very light. Five thousand shells and a half dozen wounded; usual War Department extravagance," adding after a moment, "One fatality." (I hardly conscious of the offhand memorial to torn-apart and mercifully dead young Asa); thinking, rather, of my old friend, wondering how upset he really was, upset enough to send his good sense turning end-over-end, to let him take two extra strides and lift the Captain's pistol from the unbuttoned holster?—Saying at once to myself the equivalent of "Now! Now!" in the reassuring voice of a father waking you out of a nightmare.

In reality hearing the levelheaded voice of the sergeant, in an undertone quietly to Gonzalez: "On the roof, sir," pointing. "By the lintel. Can you see him? Would the Captain permit . . .?" held-out hand finishing the question—and turning my "nightmare" in a new direction as I remembered (half remembered) the run-in, the reprimand on his record, and now the opportunity of an "accidental" balancing the score: "Don't give it to him!" on my tongue, and the pistol handed over before I could have said it—Palef bending and spreading feet for purchase and firing with both hands, the snake flipping under the log, half under it, scotched or not I couldn't tell.

And then it happened, I hardly sure to this day what it was that happened (the sequence, the who? how? why?), my mind still hearing "casualties very light. One fatality," still dimly thinking of the unintended memorial to dead Asa, all of it, I now believe (almost believe), casting a sort of prophetic ill-omened shadow ahead of the next few seconds like a scudding cloud—Palef watching the log, pistol extended, ready for another shot, Gonzalez reaching for the gun and, to my surprise, the Doctor beside him and reaching also, no words between them (between us) as if the snake might hear and take cover, Gonzalez grasping the gun barrel, or the Doctor grasping it, or Palef, everything happening so fast, in such a blur of images, such confusion of hands and fingers that whose finger was in the trigger guard is impossible to say, or whose hand the gun was in (if in any single hand), or whether it was aimed, or flapping about between the three of them, the cram-full moment overflowing with a blast of the gun that seemed louder than any of the other blasts and the Doctor spinning away from us, brushing against me, taking two or three staggering steps, left hand (or what remained of it) clutched under his right arm and already wetting his side with blood that looked brown on the khaki shirt, spots of it falling on the soft sand kicked up by our tramping.

What had happened? Clearly an accident, but what had been meant to happen? And had anyone meant anything to happen? If yes, who had meant what? All of it with me like a snapshot view from a jarred camera, no firm outlines of anything; nothing clear—or ever would be. Palef with the gun? And a chance to get even with Gonzalez? Or get even with the Doctor for talking too much? Hardly. The Doctor with the gun? Head full of jealousy? Hardly.—Accident with a pistol? It happened all the time.

Half an hour at the Post Hospital—there with Millie (and a memory of the change in her face at learning of the accident, the quick pulling together of eyebrows, the quick O of her mouth round as a dollar),—then on to the big hospital in town, he beside me under some sort of shot that left him mumbling, "No more root canals, Allen. No more needles into gums. No more mouths!", and after a silence, "Travel. Round the world, Jessie and I. Then round again, round and round," moving the white bandages an inch or two in a rotary motion and sending me a flash of our Madras hotel and myself suffering under the very freedom he rejoiced at—or pretended to, voice sinking to a sleepy tone probably muffled by his drugs: "A sad tale's best for winter," turning his head to smile at Millie leaning over to lay a hand on his shoulder. "I'll tell it softly, Millie. Yond' crickets shall not hear. A man dwelt by a churchyard . . ." voice melting out as I turned left at *Emergency Entrance*.

"What happened?" from my Alice, home again (in the little souvenir of Father's architect days), I shaking my head: "Accident with a pistol. It happens all the time."

And "accident" it remains today—tonight as I glance again at the three on the steps with snapshot smiles that bring back the ten days like the rerun of an old home movie, then flick them into the fire to flare and curl and sink in gray powder with hardly a wisp of smoke: Gonzalez, the Doctor and Jessica, Palef behind in shadow, and Millie on the porch in a glider (half my age that summer—but not today, by time's odd arithmatic; pulling my eyes to the phone as if she had rung it).

Not an indifferent tossing them away, but as you move on over a printed line from what you have read to what you haven't—or as you wander in a "churchyard" among the headstones of your contemporaries if you are an old man: Gonzalez upped to Major and transferred, the Doctor and Jessica at the Lake when not on passenger-carrying freight boats bound for "somewhere else", Millie lost to sight in the years Dark Forest; all of them burning with hardly a wisp of smoke, and turning me away from the black andirons to shuffle among the discards for another throwout—trimming down my movables—and chancing on another one with drops of rain or mist or time reflecting rainbows with ends you are promised a nice reward for finding:

My childless Alice, on her knees with gardening gloves and a trowel, white pants snug round her callipygian end, setting out a border of something at the souvenir house we bought (she bought), planting something in soil more fertile than herself (we believed at the time)—not brooding over childlessness, I thought, but maybe feeling about it as I had felt in our far-back travels about needing to measure myself among the breardwinners of the world; maybe she did want a child, to measure herself among the mothers.

Denying it once to her visiting parent who said, "You ought to have a baby, Alice."

"We don't want a baby, Mama!" exclamation point; "Why do you say such a thing?"

"Because I think you'd make such a good mother," smiling at the sewing in her lap but probably thinking of her daughter's beautiful breasts; and probably also (a foot-on-the-ground lady) of the old—now exploded—superstition current in her day about children cementing a marriage.

But childless still the evening Mary phoned from Lexington about their father: shunted aside as president of some race-horse association that meant a lot to him, voted out for a younger man—Sister Mary passing on the

news, casually, not making too much of it, a
sort of sprained-his-ankle tone; then, a few
weeks later, adding at the end of another catch-
ing-up chat, "Old man's at it again, honey."
" 'At it'?" "They stopped him driving home
from the Track. DWI, Alice."
" 'DWI'—what's that?"
"Drunk driving, baby. Where have you been
all your life?"

Alice murmuring something in a distressful
tone, and repeating it all to me when she hung
up: "Got it fixed somehow, first offense. Not in
the papers. But that's not the point. He's on the
bottle again,"—turning me to a glimpse of my
own father, about the same age and both of
them losing out on something that was impor-
tant to them; and maybe Father also replacing
one crutch he had relied on with the other
crutch that up to now had meant little to him;
not that such a prop at his age would be disaster but it would signal a sort of surrender (as
irreversible as the one at Asa's Fort that I was
writing of in my—neglected—thesis).

And childless still, I was pleased to think,
the morning Mary called again; leaving for
Kentucky was simpler than if there had been
children to provide for. Seemed to be simpler;
but began to be complicated when I called the

97

airport: no flights of any help to us until 10:12 the next morning, and even that one meant a change in Atlanta and an hour's wait.

"Hire a plane!" when I told her. "We can be there in two hours. What time is it? Where's my watch?"—on edge and annoyed, too, I had called about scheduled flights (in my pinchpenny way); and I suspect still annoyed, at possibly a more deep-rooted level, by our "words" of a week or two ago: "I saw you kissing Jessica." "Yes, Jessica seemed to want to be kissed and I kissed her." "Well, I don't like it." "But you weren't kissing her, honey." "And I'm not laughing, either!" (Reminding me, as any of our large or small discords did, of divorced Sister Mary's ridiculous, "You two are not right for each other," tapping the ash off her cigarette the way the laboratory assistant dabs at the hole in your skin from the needle. "Did Alice tell you that?" "Just a feeling," shoulders up and down, and walking off—she liked to leave a footprint.)

"Charter a plane, for God's sake! Buy a plane!" to me already in glasses thumbing through the telephone book for the small airfield for charter flights.

And reaching a clipped voice that might have been accepting Want Ads for the newspaper: "Lexington Kay Wy? Hold it." I said, "It's urgent please, Miss," (in my out-of-date way), and she said, "Hold it," and left me listening to a dreamy piped-in tune with one ear and to Alice with the other as she moved about her open suitcase on the unmade bed and said distantly, "You don't need to go, you know; I can handle it," as Miss Want-Ads came back on with, "How many passengers?" firmly, as if her computer was wasting current, and I said, "Two passengers," answering both ladies.

"Lex and return?"

I told her One way, and she said after a wait as though clearing it with her machinery, "We can provide the service you require, sir. One-way to Lexington Kay Wy, two passengers, one-prop Cessna 172, flight time approximately three hours, 334 degrees heading plus or minus wind correction. We would require one-and-one-half hours preparation notice. The charge would be eleven hundred and sixty-seven twenty payable in advance. May I ask if your check would be drawn on a local bank?"

I couldn't help saying (with my ingrained respect for money), "Eleven hundred dollars!" and she said, "And sixty-seven twenty," as Alice snapped at me, "Buy it!"

I dug up our bank-account number and gave it to her; I told her we would be at the field by one-thirty and hoped to leave before two, could she manage that? and she said, "No problem." I hung up and repeated the "No problem" to Alice to make her smile (the flip expression that year one of the little semi-jokes between us that often seemed amusing); she ignored it, going on with filling her suitcase, face as white as the underclothes she was packing.

We didn't have all the details of the matter, but Sister Mary who had phoned her, bitter herself, seemed to get some satisfaction out of sharing the grimness: their father, morose and half drunk, phoning Mrs. O'Neal visiting in Cincinnati that he was going to shoot himself, and Mrs. O'Neal telling him, "All right, but don't do it in the house."

The sister going on through Alice's "God damn the woman!", going on with a matter-of-factness that was itself almost cruel except that it was probably a way of trying to spread out the cruelty she felt she had been in the midst of, bearing alone (no husband now, the only brother buying horses in Australia, or some place): Early that morning their father had driven his car to the funeral director's back

100

door, sat down against a wall and shot himself in the mouth. "Thoughtful of him, wasn't it, Alice!" and from Alice, "God damn the man!" and breaking the connection.

Recounting the talk to me with tears more of anger than distress, the anger spreading out to include me as she disdained my show of understanding by waving wet fingers at the phone and demanding that I call the sister back about our arrangements; which I did—that we were taking a plane, would be there about five o'clock, not to meet us, we would get a taxi.

A sunny summer midday, 1:40 as we left the *Chevy* in the shade of some pine trees by the hangar, the wind sock on the field hardly lifting; not too hot, a fine day for flying even at the price, I unloading our bags, locking up and going into the office with my check for eleven hundred and sixty-seven dollars and twenty cents (my check, Alice's dollars).

A thin young man with a green baseball cap on the back of his head was at the desk gathering up some papers, nodding a yes-he-understood-all-that to a woman in bold glasses telling him, "Lex is controlled. Contact the tower for permission to land. This is your pilot, Mr.,

Mr.," glancing at my signature and managing, "Embry," the young man saying, " 'Tom,' Mr. Embry," and giving me a finger-crushing handshake.

We found Alice at a vending machine in a corner of the hangar, pulling this lever and that to no effect as you might try different excuses with an unresponsive traffic cop, rescued as we appeared by a boy in torn-off jeans, fifteen or so, who interceded, knew the buttons and pulls and where to reach, and handed up her package of chewing gum, she breaking the seal, passing him a thank-you stick and taking one herself (exchanging not smiles but twinkles perhaps). Our pilot touched a finger to his cap at seeing Alice, said, "Here we go, ma'am," and picked up one of the suitcases. I was reaching for the other when the boy seized it like a robber, and the pilot said, "Billy wants to come along for the ride?" glancing at me for an okay. Alice said, "Let him come," as if she and Billy had discussed it and I nodded, Billy giving her a hand at the door of the plane as if his mother had taught him manners (a black-haired boy about the age ours might have been—I wondering if such a thought had occurred to Alice).—My watch said ten after two, as if mumbling Right on schedule.

And twenty after, when I looked again as the tremble of our wheels melted into quiet with the seamlessness of moving from awake into sleep; or from one way of feeling to another, and I reached for her hand on the armrest in reconciliation. She moved unresponsive fingers for cigarettes in her handbag and I turned away to the window, to the houses below us without walls, the circular trees without trunks, the cars without wheels, and then to the sky-colored river like an Interstate from Tybee Light to the great mountains (from Asa's Fort to Clingmans Dome), our pilot turning upstream as if at a highway marker labeled SMOKIES and seconds later jabbing downward like a tour guide at the white spillway of a dam and a lake, then facing about to say. "Seven thousand is my best altitude but I've got a moderate head wind and I'm holding down to six until I reach the high ground," alarming me by the way he turned round to speak, the equivalent in my mind of taking your eyes off the road.

I said, "And when you come to the 'high ground'?" making a question of it (my leg muscles tightening at the memory of pushing me up something called *Gregory Bold*). Which he answered as if reading from a manual; "I'll go

up to eight-five. *Clingmans* is only six-seven.
No problem. I could go up to twelve but I don't
have oxygen—"

And some other in-house talk that faded out
for me in the reverse image his figures brought
back to me of gazing up from our mountain
cottage one summer at the now-and-then
plane crossing the open bay of sky from ridge
to ridge, appearing without a sound and halfway across before you heard it, leaving a de-
scending parachute of hum in the air after it
vanished that made me think, that summer, of
Alice leaving behind one of her fragrances as
she passed (kissing me when I told her so); our
holiday cottage at perhaps 5,000 feet and the
planes at maybe 3,000 above us—at "eight-
five"?—to cross the great walls ahead, Europe
behind us, my broken tooth repaired, myself
with a foothold among the breadwinners
(thanks, for both, to the Doctor) and already in
my head a memory of Asa and a half-formed
plan for night study and a Master's in history—

All of it fading out to now, as I watched her
transfering the chewing gum from her mouth
to a piece of Kleenex, storing it with Alice-
neatness in her handbag and opening the de-
pleted package for another stick; shaking the

package at Billy staring over his shoulder, and smiling at his pulling out a stick, folding it professionally and adding it to what was already in his mouth—the first real smile of the day and whisking me back to, "You ought to have a baby, Alice," from my mother-in-law, and "Why do you say such a thing!" and, "Because I think you'd make such a good mother" (a hint of "mother" in the smile at Billy).

The river below us more like a back-country road than an Interstate, twisting downhill to meet us, white flecks in the water from rocks and rapids, the white ribbon of a waterfall appearing and leaving behind a reminder of high land ahead, of there being no waterfalls downstream; black roads now, some white, some pink as the walls of Asa's Fort, all with more turns per mile, skirting hills defined by curved furrows like contour lines on a map—all of it seeming closer, as if the land had climbed more than we had; some cloud shadows now (the first I had noticed) moving over the fields and the woods, spreading a fading-out gray like Father with a floated-on watercolor wash— Alice facing the other window with a gaze that seemed to stop at the glass, I wondering if she would be any more aware of the great ridge when we crossed it a thousand feet below us.

And unaware, apparently, of the tissue-paper clouds in streamers beyond the window now as if the wisps had drifted lower in a mountain rain squall; or as if he had begun to climb and entered them at his "eight-five." Passing through them into sun again, and I there reading them idly as the clouds that had blown between my wife and me that would give way, I didn't doubt, to sun too—as other clouded spells had done in our years together (refuting Sister Mary's, "You two aren't right for each other," as she read us through her own marital disaster, having no conception of how my imagination went blank at the thought of what I would have left if my wife divorced me—and none at all of the prison cell for myself I could foresee at the always-present possibility of her dying before I did; the thought of it each time bringing back the moment of my chancing to pass our cemetery as a hat-in-hand young man waited at the gate for two children behind him running, laughing, playing tag among the headstones).

Love between us? What else? And yet we hardly ever used the word, kept it in reserve like special china in a corner-cabinet, except that it was more for home use than for company; not the way, I used to think, of Jessica

and the Doctor to whom it seemed more everyday than special. Sometimes asking myself
how we had managed it (she possibly asking
herself too, but neither asking the other): no
children holding us together, and even if there
had been, the little creatures have lost most of
their binding power for the up-to-date house-
hold. Money? But I was a breadwinner now
(some crumbs, anyway); I didn't need to have
a rich wife. Biology? But sensuality wears
down fast, will snap out on you like an overage
fan belt.—What could it be between us but
love? We had disagreements, differences of
taste, surface things, but beneath them all was
a sort of interlocking, a two-way reliance, con-
sideration, an unemphasized acceptance of
tending "this" together, of lifting it but also
being lifted by it. Incomprehensible, I feel, to
people today, hooked on more run-of-the-mill
injections; incomprehensible to my sister-in-
law—I wondering sometimes if I could offer
her an explanation she would understand by
mentioning our now-and-then decision (con-
veyed by eyes or hands or shoulders or I can't
say what) to sink a bottle of good champagne
in our ice bucket and alternate its lovely
edginess with bites of toasted poundcake until
we were shoeless and shirtless and pantsless

and dancing to What's-his-name on the phonograph (the clarinet fellow)—

"Seat belts, folks; I'm going up to seven-five," over his shoulder—not turning his head this time, as if not to lose his place in reading the streamer clouds in front of him, wipers fanning like metronomes (counting off the time-clouds between this moment and the clarinet player, Benny Something—Goodman!).

She didn't move and I said, "Buckle up, baby, he's coming to the big stuff," she making no sign of hearing me, gazing at the clouds, or just the glass, or at the jumble of things in her head from the phone calls (a jumble I thought of as odds-and-ends thrown into a hasty bundle—some anger, some distress, some general emotional tightness that didn't have a place for me one way or another). Fastening the seat belt for her was like pulling up the blanket over Alice-sleeping, but she touched my hand when I finished and it made me think of the Coast and getting a postcard from her in Kentucky after a week's silence.

Actually brought back another faraway moment of dismissing annoyance at something I had done, seemed to have done: driving south from Paris in a yellow dix-cheveaux, headed for Italy—any place but Paris after what had happened—windshield wipers brushing at the rain; brushing at the time-clouds between now and then. And revealing Madame Levrile our landlady who couldn't understand our coming from the South in America without coming from South America, and her daughters Celeste and Nadine who understood that and also understood the ways of the world well enough to misinterpret the little episode that had annoyed my wife.

I had found an apartment to retreat to, planning to straighten out some notes on our travels I had accumulated, as well as to escape from Madame (to say nothing of the burning-with-curiosity daughters); a sublet for a month from a Monsieur Carbie while he took a trip to Germany—the rental alone, in advance, providing him with grand-luxe accomodations: ten minutes up a Paris avenue, passing under a Paris marquee brightly blinking TROIS JEUNNES FILLES NUES (which meant nothing to me, having one for my very own) and on to my garçonniére in a new building, third floor, elevator, beautiful place; sofas, easy chairs, rugs, bathroom, kitchenette. I invited them all to a moving-in party, Alice, Celeste, Nadine, Madame (she declined). I was putting the champagne in the ice bucket when I heard the elevator; I remembered I had forgotten to unlock the door, but my hands were wet and I went to the kitchen for a towel.

When I came back a young woman had opened the door with a key and was staring at me in caught-breath astonishment (through our caught-breath astonishments, you might say); silence between us like an opaque curtain, ending at last with "M'sieu Carbie, il n'est pas ici?" glancing right and left as if he were hiding. I said in my crippled French that Monsieur Carbie was in Germany, I was renting the apartment for a month, please come in, I was having a few friends. (Thoroughly invitable, incidentally: navy blue beret slanted at an angle that suggested mirrors and turnings of the head, a tailored jacket with an ornament in the lapel, a small leather bag on a shoulder strap.) She glanced about, asked without much accent if I had found everything I needed; "There are nicer glasses in the pantry cabinet," frowning at the ones I had selected—as my three guests walked in from the elevator, Alice staring, Celeste and Nadine sharing raised-eyebrow smiles that said they had known all along what M'sieu was up to.

I said, "Mad'moiselle is looking for Monsieur Carbie," but it was no use.—I turned in the keys and we packed up and set out for Italy; in the rain and glum. On the outskirts of town she clearing the air by touching my hand and laughing, asking me how much rent had gone down the drain (respectful of money—we both were)—

Rain now shifting from our dix-cheveaux windshield to the plane window at my elbow, fog beyond it like a cool steam, clouds evidently no thinner at "seven-five" than at six. Making me wonder if he would climb again, "go up to eight-five" (the way I had recently gone upstairs at the school to escape a persistent complainer of grades), glancing over his shoulder with something like "Up again, folks" or just go on "up", saying nothing, letting us get the message by the push on the back of our shoulders.

But he was seeing something we didn't see, or not seeing what he wanted to see.—The next minute, or two minutes, or however long the "minute" lasted, took me back half-a-hundred years to a childhood moment at the seacoast (by Tybee Light), wading in the quiet fringe of surf, the foaming friendly sheet of spent waves, ignoring the three thousand miles of indifferent might behind me, and being lifted and twisted and tumbled in a curling green breaker out of nowhere—up and on one wing and round at the instant of seeing a wall of dripping stone beyond the window at a slant that made you wonder where was up, where down, seat belt straining across my middle, the rest of me floating up from the seat as if inflated, a sucking gasp from my wife (or from myself) as I reached for her arm—or she reached for mine—no words between us, no breath for words; and no words out of the pilot, but a new sound from the motor as if responding to words, to an order, and a banking turn and dip and leveling, and an easing in the grip of my seat belt and, as if wrapped in the new air I pulled into my chest, a gliding down out of the overcast into a view of farmland in a valley passing below us at the speed of a dream, the whole tumbling moment like the twisting back somersault of the lady diver at a county fair.

"What happened?" "Where am I?" "Are you all right?" "I don't know," answering or asking, she or I or both of us. "Yes. I think. Yes," hands clutching; "Yes. Okay." And, "Sorry, folks!" over the seat-back in front of us, voice somehow retaining a memo of the chilly instants he had just passed through, the fields close below us now, peeling under us and after a triangle of flat cornfield slanting up into gray hills, his eyes studying them as if reading fine print.

"Going in, folks. Mind your belts," as he tilted and turned and passed again over the fields, some planted, some fallow, some in left-over weeds, seemed to see something worth pointing at to Billy (that might have been a stretch of split-rail fence he didn't like), then tilted and repeated the whole searching flyover, turned again over the hills and settled into the short stubble with a scratching sound against the bottom of the plane that brought back to me an instant of Asa telling of dragging his batteau over the stiff seaweed.

He faced his windshield, wipers still flapping but he didn't seem to be seeing them, seemed to put his whole mind on filling his chest with air, lifting his shoulders with a tied-in lifting of his chin and a rolling up of his eyes, saying nothing for a minute then, "Sorry, folks," again and wiping the back of his wrist across his forehead; even his sunburned neck seemed a paler brown.

On the ground, looking about him into the haze on the slopes that gave you a feeling of being under a tent, "I don't like mountains when you can't see where they are."

I asked him could he get up out of all this—

113

meaning could he get *us* up out of all this and on with our dismal errand to Lex Kay Wy— waving at the field, the weeds, the zigzag fence; he saying he wasn't worried about "this" as much as "that," with a lift of his head at the overcast and a mumble of something about clouds in the mountains; "May blow off in an hour, may hang on for a week," which I was glad Alice didn't seem to hear. I asked if he could take us back to the airport (better to return to base, with all the delay, than wait there hoping for a change in the weather— which was changing in the wrong direction, Alice moving against the body of the plane out of the misty rain beginning to fall).

He seemed about to answer but looked away, and I followed his eyes to a pickup truck bouncing down a rocky trail as if expecting ambulance work, and in any case glad for the interruption to an uneventful day.

Socializing that I thought would never end, then a lean mountaineer in bib overalls smelling of ashes—Mr. Forney—drove us, Alice and me, twenty miles in the rain to the narrow-gauge at Balsam Gap, all of us in the cab of the pickup (double-barrel on hooks at the back of our necks), suitcases behind under wet canvas, wet collie swaying on the twists of the road, the trail, with his tongue dripping spit, or rain. "Balsam's a flag stop but he'll likely pull up."

I said, " 'Likely'!"

He said, "Business slack, he be glad to see you, Jones his name, Mike Jones, we call him 'Casey' "—Alice turning over my wrist to see the time; nearly five o'clock (we should have been hailing a taxi at the Lexington airport but we didn't say so, understood without saying it). He asked us which way we were headed and when I told him Kentucky said we were in luck, Casey would put us in Boone City by suppertime and we could catch *The Sunland*. "She stops a minute about midnight."

I said, "We're in luck, baby,—if you hadn't noticed," and kissed my wife's hot cheek to bolster my weak fun; she gripped my hand and held it, and I felt as if we were finding (re-finding) a valuable something we had mislaid, as if all this shakeup in our day-to-dayness had brought to the surface an awareness we had let dim, a consciousness of what we had made between us that we had lost sight of—bringing back to me Sister Mary and her "You two aren't right for each other" and disproving it; refuting it in the inarticulate deeps of "us two," for

115

when I kissed her cheek again she turned her face and kissed me on the mouth, and the day's frustrations seemed to melt away for both of us, leaving us (me, certainly) hardly hearing, "He generally don't come through till about quarter to six. He'll more'n likely stop. Be glad to see a passenger."

Glad or not, he took us in: five wet resin-smelling flat cars of mountain timber and a half-baggage-half-passenger car, rolling by us at a disheartening speed then making a grinding stop as if he had changed his mind; no passengers, but a baggageman-brakeman-conductor in a stiff-sided cap who lifted the lady up the high step as if she were a six-year-old (managed to free a lingering eye for the stockings under the stretched hem of her skirt, that I sympathized with, understood in a man-to-man way—the instant stirring up in me a vision of the sleeping cars on the midnight *Sunland* and joining the lady in one of the berths), my vision interrupted by the sound of a plane going over, hidden in the overcast but fading out to the low lands and probably our pilot; it reminded me of a line in the old railroad song, *He was goin down grade, Makin nanty miles an hour*—which I tried to amuse Alice by repeat-

116

ing, but her background was horses not trains (and rather desperate as fun anyway).

The baggageman-brakeman-conductor succeeded better than I had, joining us like a host in the empty passenger-half and, from the armrest of the seat across the aisle, parading mountain anecdotes as he would introduce distant in-laws at a family reunion, Alice listening with more than courtesy (glad to be reminded, I thought, of the turning world beyond the grim one we were headed for): the mountain family crowding to the door of the cabin to watch the wagon go by twice a week with bark for the tannery, the old man saying, "It must be mighty lonesome for them folks back in the hills don't live on a big road"; and when it developed I was a schoolman, going on to, "Professor on the train one day, sitting right where you are, Miss, going to Highland Falls. Been teaching in one of them one-room schools up there in the Gap. Said he read the boys and girls about a man thought his missus might be two-timing him, choked her with a pillow. Said a boy got up, said, 'Look like to me, Professor, that man ought to found out for sure before he choked that lady.' "

Alice asked him if the lady's name was Des-

demona, but he said he didn't rightly recall the
professor said her name—the brakes grabbing
and lifting him to his feet for outside duties
while Casey shifted and jolted and clanged
into the couplings of more flat cars of mountain logs.

But back when we were moving again, dripping rain and with a smell of turpentine (that
flashed me back an instant visit to Father's studio, to "turps"—The Paintery), and going on
with talk I don't remember, peering at last
through the misty window and standing up
with, "He's coming in now. Pleased to visit
with you, Ma'am, and you, sir. Have a nice
holiday, both you-all."—I thanked him for his
good wishes, couldn't quite say, Thanks for
the lift in our spirits, in my wife's particularly. . . .

"Section Five," from the Pullman Conductor
bending and tearing our tickets on the light-
streaked platform beside the midnight L-&-N;
and, "Section Five," to his porter hospitable
with our baggage, and, "All aboard, please," to
us.

Falling into the lower berth, both of us—
toppled into it by the Tennessee curves and the
tilting floor that left you pushing flat-handed
against any upright you could reach then top-

pled you over into the puffed-up pillows—and into sleep waiting for us like a body-temperature pool of buoyant nothingness.

And after what seemed to me seconds, rising out of it into the dim light of our lamp as if pulled up by the long, bending, mountain-country whistle of the engine (engines?) that seemed more of a horn than a whistle, seemed a way of putting into sound the swinging motion of the berth, making it sway as if rocking an almost-still hammock between trees.

Alice by the window with the shade up six inches watching the rain that you couldn't hear, could only see in pelted white handfuls reflected in our lamplight—watching, maybe, for the bending mountain whistle in her memory, as you listen at a concert for a long cello-note to return. I kissed her for the memories we shared, for the dangers we had passed, and she kissed me that I remembered, turning away from them, and the thought of them, and the rain on the window, and looking at me as if through the curves and twists of the day and their way of separating the day from those before and those ahead, forced against me by a mountain curve and over me as if I were one of her horses, knees holding her on, tilting with the sway of the car and falling over my neck as

119

if to save herself a spill—all of our day seeming to repeat itself in miniature, our tension and release as if patterned on the twisting tumbling movement of the plane, lifting up in a breathless tilt and after a timeless moment level again and sliding down and landing; escaping that death (and this one) and escaping, then and now, all memory of the one in Lexington—and all thought of the one out there ahead somewhere for the two of us, all of them ignored, forgotten, wiped away in a rainbow arc with death at one end, the far end, and life at the other, the near.

For she phoned me at home from Lexington (I had gone to the funeral—the family as composed as if dropping a parcel in a street-corner mailbox—and crossed the rainy mountains at 36,000 feet), said before saying anything else, "I thought it would never happen, but it has," with the smile in her voice of at last proving herself among the mothers.—And, home again, smiling, "If you like," to my proposal of "Ada" as a possible name, for its reminder of Asa.

And in no time, Ada O'Neal Embry was in Paris on her "Junior Year Abroad"! Not only in Paris but at Madame Levrile's, sent there for old-time's sake (Madame long gone but spin-

ster daughters taking in two or three special
"guests" from here and there, one, for a week
or two, "from South America"—Alabama).—
Snapshots somewhere of all this "no time" but
not at hand for the flames between the black
andirons, leaving me to turn away and shuffle
among the discards for other throwouts—trimming down my movables.


And come on: Father in a canvas cap on the
seat of a tractor talking to a black man on the
ground, sawed-off pines behind him, stumps
bright with bleeding beads of resin (a few new-
planted forest trees, six or eight feet tall); visor
of the cap at a slant, not rakish, only neglectful,
only to keep off the July sun while he trans-
formed the country place, "Five Springs," into
his Shangri-La, or meant to.—At seventy-six!
    We laughing at him: "Put your feet up, Papa.
Enjoy yourself. You've worked hard all your
life, done a good job." (Wasting your breath.)
    No snapshots of him in the twenty years
before—except in our heads: selling his part-
nership in the architecture firm and setting out
for New York and the Art Students League at
fifty-six to do what he had "always wanted to
do" (Mama rolling her eyes at the ceiling but

getting out the suitcases); through all the
school years of mail-order courses in drawing
I've heard him talk about, fat envelopes in his
mailbox more waited-for than letters from
home.

Telling me once (more than once) about
painting in a class at college under an old professor back from Italy. " 'Whom do you paint
for?' ", says the old man (somebody had asked
the question—probably with a "who"); "You
paint for the person who knows the most
about it," as he shifted scraps of colored cloth
about in front of little mirrors on a table. "And
you work to make that person yourself."

And I saying, "Quite an earful, Papa, at
nineteen," or some such thing, back from our
wanderings, Alice and I, and often stopping by
his "Paintery" (not "Studio," by some quirk of
his own).

Dropping it all for architecture, "a sort of
second cousin once removed, Miss Alice";
heavy going until he landed something in the
drafting room of Walker-Baker-Taylor AIA that
in time became Taylor-Embry, and eventually
Taylor & Taylor when he sold out after thirty
years: "Retiring at fifty-five, Peter!" from one
after another in the firm.—Of course he wasn't
"retiring" at all; he was more like the man in

the fable coming home to marry his high-school sweetheart.

Summer after summer among the New York painters (Mama with him, no small children now, summers hot in Georgia. He said at first the girls bothered him and I said, "What do you mean, Papa? The girls tried to pick you up?" (I liked to tease him). He said, "I used to turn my head and look at the skylight while they came in and stood there without a stitch waiting to be told what to do." I said, "But Papa, you were fifty-five years old!"

He said, "Fifty-seven," and I said, "And you'd never seen a naked girl before?"

He said he got used to them after a while, said one of them at Cranbrook forgot the pose after a "take-ten", couldn't find the monitor and asked him where her left hand had been. He told her on the front of her upper leg (she was sitting). She said, "Here?" He said, "No, higher," and she said, "Show me, Dad."

"And you showed her, Papa?" "Of course I showed her!" "Showed her from the painting you were working on?" "I picked up her hand and put it where it belonged." I said, "Higher up on her leg, Papa?" and he told me to get out, he was busy.

Busy at paintings, oils and watercolors, busy

at fumbling through his memory as if for discards to feed a fire of his own; telling us once
(Alice and me, on a drop-in visit—Ada at kin-
dergarten, I believe), "Old man once sat down
by me in the shade, down in Texas somewhere, don't remember where. I was painting
a family of cactus plants, arms reaching up
praying for rain. He said, 'Let me ask you
something, Mr. Painterman,' and went on to
talk about 'all those French pictures a few years
ago up in New York and Chicago,' said, 'They
made everybody so mad they had to call out
the police.' I told him I hadn't seen the show
but I had seen some of the pictures in France
before the War, and he said, 'Before the War!
That's what I'm taling about. People get to be
like the people in the pictures. These sharp-
eyed painter boys, they'd seen all that war
trouble coming for twenty years. Pictures used
to have some peace and quiet—naked girls at a
picnic on the grass, going swimming with
nothing on, nice pictures, made you feel good.
Then the painter fellows got uneasy and began
to scatter and shatter and disintegrate. That
sister with both eyes on one side of her face,
she's scared, mister. And that one on the stairs,
she's all to pieces, shaking like a Zepperlin's
dropped a bomb in the next street. But when

that boy painted her everybody was saying war was outdated, something for the history books. And he didn't *see* any war coming. Just maybe felt a little shaky one day, and painted that trembling woman. This war's breaking up the world into a Cubist picture. But the pictures were painted ten or fifteen years ago.'— What do you make of that, Allen?"

I said, "Papa, are you aiming to be a prophet and a painter too?" and he said, "They're hand-in-glove, Allen,"—and I felt like Mama when she looks at the ceiling with that leave-him-alone-he's-not-hurting-anybody look.

Oils, watercolors, drawings, going at them, it seemed to me, with his mind more on the *how* than the *what*. "It's not subject-matter that makes the picture. You're painting a relationship of picture elements, you're asking them what they want to be," throwing a ragged charcoal line on a sheet of heavy paper, crossing it with another, and another, and after a time filling an area with gray from a charcoal stick on its side, I saying, "But Papa, what about all those naked girls you painted—after putting their hands back on their upper legs?" which he ignored, studying the shapes with what seemed satisfaction and turning away to us with, "Thad Suits used to say, 'Confucius say, "Idea present, brush may return to pocket," ' " watching it from an angle, then saying with a down-the-years smile that some old people can manage, "Delightful fellow."

I said, "Confucius?" and he said, "Suits.— Delightful people. Dan Lutz used to run a few scales on his bassoon while his watercolor dried—" And so on.

Not my field but I liked to hear him talk about painting, the adopted center of his life that was like a foster child that appealed to you more than your own (as we used to think might happen, in our pre-Ada years).

When he said, "Lamar said, 'Takes two to paint a picture, one to start it, one to stop it,' " Alice said, " 'Idea present, brush may return to pocket'?" and we all laughed, I excessively perhaps, pleased at my Alice's neat refitting it.

"Russel Green used to say, ' "Art for art's sake"? Bullhockey! Art for God's sake.'—Delightful people. There's something about drawing and painting, Miss Alice, that makes for good-feeling. Your inside life coming out through your hands and arms and eyes—" And on and on (giving me a sort of kindly worry as to his being, as we say, "all there").

Alice sent me a let-him-alone signal and we wandered out on to a balcony he had and sat down on a bench. When we came back he was floating a sky-blue color on the slanted paper with a bristle brush and a purplish red that he splashed on with a smaller brush, tilting the paper and letting the red fade into the whites in some places and into the blues.

I said, "But Papa, what *is* it?" and he said, as if he hadn't thought of that, "Well, it's a venture, Allen. Like a young human being. Like your charming little Ada, if you please. You don't *know* what they'll grow into; you give them some background and some guiding principles, and hope," fastening the paper to a board with clamps at the corners.

I said, "But, my God, Papa, you're doing it all backwards," he laughing a little and reciting, " 'Let there be light' " (floating the backs of his fingers over the white areas as if sowing "light"). "Then let there be colors in the light. Then let the colors show living shapes, male and female—Adam and Eve," smiling at me and adding, "It's a time-honored procedure, Allen."

I said, "But Papa, you're not the Lord God Jehovah!" Alice nudging me with an elbow—and Mama at home shaking her head with her look of let-him-be-he's-not-hurting-anybody.

Pictures by the hundreds; in oil colors, water

colors, drawings and washes in ink (Chinese, India, American). Persuading the local art association to hang thirty or forty in its galllery, then renting other galleries too and hanging enough more to feel justified in calling the display "74-AT-74" and mailing out a basketful of invitations (most of them in Alice's neat script). "What about prices, Mr. Peter?"

"Prices, honey?" waving both hands; and she filling out the price tags representing the composite attitudes of the family: $100, $125, $150—which his sparce and whispering attendance found forbidding, and we brought them back, all "74," to hang on his walls at home and at the Paintery and on our walls now that we were settled in a place of our own. Mama accepting them complacently until wall space began to run out and he proposed hanging them one above another: "This is not the Louvre, Peter!" but steadying the ladder and the calves of his seventy-five-year-old legs that shouldn't have been on the ladder in the first place.—A one-way enterprise: production for a clientele that didn't exist (except that they weren't *for* a clientele but were pushed out of him from inside like your fingernails, your hair).

"I'm leaving them all to the College," I heard him explain to divorced Sister Mary on a visit

to us from Kentucky. "I don't want the estate
people coming in here when I'm gone and
running up the inheritance taxes by appraising
them at some fabulous figure," Sister Mary
having enough left-over rancor from her divorce to say with a nice smile that she didn't
think he needed to worry.

I doubt if Papa heard her estimate of his
work (though he did give up the College idea),
saying to me a few days later, "Why has everybody started mumbling, Allen? You can't understand half they say—not that you miss
much." I told him people usually mumbled;
which he didn't accept, saying, "You mean it's
my ears?" a little offended, as if I had spoken ill
of the *356 Porsche*.

Of course it was his ears, his hearing, and of
course it underlined the growing sense of remoteness that I thought had moved him step
by step away from the everyday world and
eventually landed him in the Paintery among
the abandoned cotton warehouses—and
among the elastic memories of seventy years
before: "That window over there in the old
Cotton Exchange was my grandfather's office
in 1910," pointing it out for Alice from his
balcony, fingers black with Chinese ink.
"When I remember the old man was six years

129

younger than I am today it gives me a sort of genealogical acrophobia like looking over into the Grand Canyon," smiling at Alice, who smiled back (they got along well together—I had heard it all before).

And down, it seemed, into the Canyon itself with a trip one Sunday to the old place in the country, "Five Springs," almost nothing left of it but the springs, as persistent in flow as himself; the big square house long burned to the ground, nothing left of it except in his mind.

"Father was a bell man" (in the sense of somebody crazy about bells), our picnic spread out on some blankets on the ground, all of us and the Doctor and Jessica—back for a time from their wanderings. "That one," leading us inside what was left of the barn and pointing at a wide-skirted bell on a chain from a beam; "Father bought it for three dollars when the monkeys tore down the old courthouse," the Doctor pulling the rope on the clapper with his good hand and releasing waves of bronze reverberations that beat about the stalls and mangers like great birds. "And this one came off the old firehouse in the days of hook-and-ladders and steamers and galloping horses. . . ."

And "this one" and "that one," leading us about the barn like a guide in a museum of

130

sounds, pulling and releasing the clappers and smiling at us as if watching us taste the deep pulses—watching Alice (a little sensitive, I believe, about showing her the run-down old place against his picture of her bluegrass Kentucky horse-pastures).

Silent for a while over Mama's stuffed eggs, which he liked, then looking off among the slopes and weedy fields and saying if he didn't have so many pictures in his mind he had to paint he "might just come out here with a tractor and a back-hoe and pull this place together, hang those bells in the open air where they belong. Hang one of them up there by the graveyard," gesturing with one of Alice's thin sandwiches at the castiron fence and the three or four gravestones in the old cemetery, cedars standing at the gate like discreet funeral directors (an inscribed stone for Asa, but I don't think he is buried there).

Often interrupting others—not quite sure we were talking, I suppose—and breaking in now with "Charlie" in the wagon off to meet the train "and pick up ice from town in sacks of sawdust. 'Don't thow em in the sun, please, mister!' The baggageman kicking them out any old where and waving good-bye with his canvas glove" (glancing at Alice to see if she was listening). "Allen, that's a bold stream down there if it's cleared out right. Runs into Sweetwater Creek."

I couldn't help mumbling, "Sweet water, run softly till I end my song" (stupid of me, but I had been reading such things to my impervious class as late as Friday). He said, "What did you say, Allen? My ears ain't what they were"—often reaching out for "ain'ts" as he would for emphasis with his Chinese-ink sticks, and this time adding quietly, "Nor my eyes, in fact. The left one."

An operation on the eye didn't help much. Or at all, as far as painting was concerned, leaving him with a one-eyed approach to his work that shook him in a way that made me think of a circus performer losing his pole on the high-wire—the rest of us gasping from below at the sudden prospect of disaster (particularly myself with my memory of Alice's father "losing his pole" in Kentucky—bringing on a surrender for each of them as irreversible as the one at Asa's Fort I was writing of in my, neglected, thesis).

And "surrender" was the word that entered my head when I opened the door of the Paintery a few weeks after the operation: ripped-apart watercolors scattered over the floor, torn-up drawings, sketchbooks; he had a patch over the bad eye but the other one seemed quite okay for handling the destruction.

I said, "Hold everything, Papa!"

"The Art Club people are sending for the easels, the stretchers and all that. What they don't want—

I said, "Wait a minute, Papa. Let's not jump the gun. The eye-man said—"

"I know what the eye-man said. I can drive a car. And if I can drive the 356 I can sure drive the pickup. And can sure drive a tractor," his voice now with something of the gesture of the high-wire man's triumph on completing his walk. "Went out to the Springs yesterday with Stokes."

I said, " 'Stokes?' " and he said, "Best man we ever had on field jobs in the old days—except on Monday. They let him go, getting old, what not. Truth is Stokes always had a Monday problem. I'd say to him on Monday, 'Stokes, you were drunk all day yesterday.' He'd say, 'Mr. Peter, how could I been drunk I was supposed to be in church?'—We went out there to look at what's got to be done to the country place."

And so I took the picture of him on the tractor talking to Stokes on the ground, bulldozing out his Shangri-La as he created a sort of blend between architecture and the abandoned patterns of shapes and colors in his "Paintery," carving out a sort of sculpture in the Georgia clay, in the bronze waves of his re-hung bells.

Anyway, whatever he thought he was doing, off to doing it in the *356* as if the early wet slopes belonged to one of his watercolors that had to be dealt with before it dried; a couple of sandwiches apiece in a World War I musette bag with a thermos of coffee. "Water, Peter?" from Mama. "Water, honey! We've got five good springs of water"—all of it there in the magic depths of the black-and-white snapshot (in my hand resisting my commonsense impulse to burn it with others).

No photo of him with the six-foot trees, holding them vertical in the mud while Stokes fed in the topsoil, tramped it down. "Carya ovata, Allen. Shellbark Hickory." "Okay, Papa, but—" "And that's a Kentucky Coffee Tree, Miss Alice, Gymnocladus dioica." "But Papa, they're just six feet tall."

He said he had read somewhere—probably one of those Chinese people that knows everything—you planted a tree for somebody else to sit in the shade of. "That's an English Walnut. . . ."

And no photo of him in the dim light of his bedroom after they repaired his hip (broken in a tumble off the tractor that the medical people indicated to me was tied to some sort of coronary problem); Stokes there in the dim room with him most of the time, almost invisible in the shadows, listening to his grumbles—or silent anyway, nodding his head in agreement now and then, Mama and Alice looking in from time to time, with telephoned inquiries, How was he today? How was he getting on?

"Who phoned? Crosby again?"

"Didn't say who, just 'a friend.' And somebody else called this morning; I told you. Nice of them, Peter. Nice to have so many friends asking about you." He turning to Stokes with, "They're asking about our *356*, Stokes, wondering how much longer before they can get hold of our *356*."—I think I saw a bottle and two shot glasses under a corner of the bed one day, but the light was bad.

"Totally unacceptable, Allen," a week before we buried him inside the castiron fence in the country.

I said, "What is, Papa?" sure he had stumbled on my plan for burying the paintings in the movers' warehouse-sepulcher.

"Unacceptable that all this wonderful complexity should be the result of some gigantic cosmic accident."

"I wouldn't worry about it, Papa."

"And just as unacceptable that it should be the masterwork of some Great Artist 'up there.'—Totally unacceptable! It's like when somebody asks you, 'What *is* it?' about a just-begun picture. Truth is, we're not smart enough yet to catch on to what it is."

"Could be, Papa," (Stokes tilting his head at the downstairs ringing of probably another inquiry about the *356*). . . .

Burn the snapshot with the others? Of course. Yes, burn it!


And I did; fumbling another one out of the discards behind me—another one with "drops of rain, spray or mist" reflecting rainbows with ends you are promised a nice reward for finding: my tolerant-of-the-camera Alice, looking down at me with an if-you-must smile, carved-out rock steps below and on up beyond her head; loose cotton dress, socks, rubber-soled shoes, small cloth hat with a circular pin on the left quarter: Mesa Verde.

Stopping off from our holiday circuit of the Parks but really less concerned about cliff dwellings than the mail that might be waiting for us at this first forwarding address since home: up and down trails, ladders, ancient cut-out stairways to high caverns of white stone buildings like ragged teeth; running commentary by agile young men in flat-brim-med hats, "Stone-age people, basket makers, potters, . . . Mind your step, ma'am, . . . Yes, sir, that's a kiva, a sort of church. Careful on the ladder, sir," and down into a circular cave with a black hole in the center and, "Door to the Underworld, . . ." hearing him but as if his words, and the caves too, were coming through Ada's postcard we had been handed at the Lodge: bits of her "Year" (not much), "Celeste sends best wishes," and such things, off-hand, in her tight penmanship ("Celeste"?— oh yes, Madame's eldest, now running the place). "Brought in a friend from 'South America' (Alabama, if you please!)." Crowding in a PS for "Dad" (not one of our words,—and sig-naling emancipation?), "Your theater down the street with 'Trois Jeunes Filles Nues' that you

137

failed to visit—or claim you did. Marquee now
reads 'Cinq Jeunes Filles Nues.' Inflation
everywhere! We investigated, this 'South
American' and I. 'Nues' indeed, mes cher-
ies!—Á bientôt."

Which we passed back and forth between us
after supper, in our room (and in our glasses),
our window full of the tom-tom drums of the
modern-day cliff dwellers putting on a show
for the guests by a campfire below, my wife
saying, "I hope she knows more about the wild
world than I did at that age," and I saying,
"But, honey, you knew enough to grab me."

"Grab you!" but laughing; then putting
down her glasses, "This place makes me
sleepy," the summer air turning sharp through
the window.

I looked over at her in the other bed and
asked her if she was sorry she had grabbed me;
"Sister Mary always said we weren't—"

"Mary's bitter. Go to sleep."

And I did; but sleeping among ladders and
kivas and black holes in the ground with crumbling rims and stones falling interminably into
Underworlds. All of it with me through an
afternoon of hot high-altitude sunlight to a moment that I think of now as part of my night-
time worries, as predicting a black hole in my

up-to-then overall well-being (not particularly superstitious, but maybe inheriting some of Father's readiness to foresee endless possibilities in just-begun paintings—not to mention sympathizing with the famous young man cautioning his friend against thinking his philosophy contained all the answers). But it seems to me now, looking back—beyond the smoke of the discards smoldering in the ashes—that my good luck up to then was beginning to corrode.

Nothing of all that to be foreseen in the expedition itself: half-a-dozen cars trailing the ranger's up and around, and around and up, to a high level area at last of black dead pines in a blackened burned-over space with an edge looking out on valleys and streams and far-off bordering mountains; and down on nearer cliffs and caves and the rigid ancient masonry put together in the time of Mohammed and Pope Gregory the Great.

No photo of it to be discarded—except in my head—and except the sort of audio-photo of the ranger's, "Lightning likes this place," glancing about at the burned trees, some standing, some prostrate. "Something in the soil, iron ore maybe." One of our group with the holiday camera of a banker on his chest said, "Gold? Gold draws lightning," and the ranger, as if he had dealt with the suggestion a hundred times, "We haven't run down any yet," everybody smiling and following him off along the edges, he pointing at this and that among the valley cliffs; but lifting his head now and then I thought to check on the clouds building up over the ridges as if they had been a pack of dogs that might be friendly or might not.

Alice mumbling at me in the midst of his, "Painted designs in many rooms . . ." and such guide-book details (showing where her mind was), "You didn't invite *me* to the Trois Jeunes Filles Nues." I mumbled back that I didn't go to see them myself, that I already had one jeune fille nue, and she laughed, taking my hand—both of us turning heads toward the valley and a sustained mumble of thunder, that seemed to speak to the ranger like signal drums to his ancient Indians. He called out, "All right, everybody, we're moving on, please," pointing at the cars, looking right and left as if counting his brood then moving up the rim of the drop-off toward wanderers who hadn't heard him, or weren't ready to leave (the "banker" kicking about in the burned-over soil as if for a nugget, his ladies watching the new light patterns in the valley as the clouds climbed over the sun).

Alice gave no sign of hearing him, speaking after a moment as if still with her ghosts of Paris: "I don't feel too good about our child, Allen." I asking Why, (as though the thought was new to me), and she adding in a voice that seemed meant for herself, "School, college, she's been away so long. Who is she, by now? . . ."

"We're moving on, please, everybody—" the rest of it lost in a flash over the valley like a short circuit and a close-coupled bowling-alley tumble of thunder, the ranger raising his voice into a level that suggested he might have been a drill sergeant not many years ago: "Everybody out! Here we go, folks!" waving at the cars, moving toward his own, opening the door when he got there and waiting.

His "folks" not much concerned, talking among themselves, pointing at streaks of far sun in the valley, sorry to leave (except Alice and me, less preoccupied with the place—I'd say—than with "our child" and her Junior-Year-Abroad), as a bright shaft of lightning stabbed into the trees like a spear of one of the cliff-dwelling hunters. A shake-up then among us all as if the flash had thrown a light into dangerous corners we hadn't reckoned on; not much response in words but a fusillade of banging car doors, grinding starters, motors catching, and for me a faint smell in the air that tied me back to streetcars and trolleys popping sparks, and then a smell of fresh pine smoke.

"Straight out to the highway and left!" from the ranger, arms like a traffic cop's, Alice running, tripping on a fallen branch or root or leaf-hidden hole, tumbling to her knees-elbows-forehead and lying there stunned, unable to get up until I could reach her, then unable to stand, to touch her left foot to the ground, the ranger wheeling his car over the underbrush and beside us as the rain began. . . .

Twenty miles to a neat little hospital in Cortez, the leg straight out on a suitcase in a bandage by the roomclerk at the Lodge (who had handed us our mail). Cortez, and a gentle young man with a stethoscope in his white pocket injected something to quiet her pain; and sent us on a hundred miles to Dr. Some-body a bone-man in the hospital at Gallup, mumbling to me through his trimmed brown beard, "We may have a fractured fibula here. Maybe not. His pictures'll tell him." I thanked him, asked for his bill, he shaking his head with "NC. Good luck," and rolling the wheelchair to the car in person.

Ten days in Gallup that seemed a month, then Alice forcing thank-you smiles for the nurses and turning her whole attention to managing the crutches and to getting herself and them into the car (oblivious of the wash-wax job I had bought in celebration of her dismissal—and of the might-have-been-worse appraisal I gave it that so much of our overall good fortune was still intact). I said, "It might have been worse, baby," and she said, "How?" with an edgy laugh at the windshield.

Two weeks in Santa Fe; postponing the 1500 miles of driving home, getting in and out of the car a dozen times, managing the "walker," which she now liked better than the crutches— or despised less.

But five days on the road and home again at last; more talks with medical people, more "pictures," more nods of satisfaction, she moving about by then on a pair of canes with a concentrated attention that reminded me of our Ada at 2 learning to walk.

And on one cane, carefully, doubtfully, by the time she got the envelope with the West German stamps and the letter from Sister

Mary traveling with a widow (or divorced) friend: this and that—when she read it aloud after a "Listen to this!" in a non-Alice voice— then, " 'Who should we see in a plush restaurant on the Avenue George V but your dear little Ada! And with a friend, please! Introduced him, Bruce Somebody, writes things. Well-tailored, urbane, even suave, and, my dear, coal black! We stopped only a minute, obviously de trop—' "

Alice looking up through her glasses then taking them off to see me better, silent for a moment in a silence of blocked words, then swallowing and reading on of Mary asking Ada to the hotel: " 'A brief but very nice visit. She seems well, looks well, pretty as ever. Said Bruce was famous, "though maybe not to you" (don't you like that! Ignorant old horsey aunt!). Said he had moved to France where his color was "not a liability but an asset, like a sunburn." Said she was planning to drop out of college, live in Europe—' "

I said, "Now wait a minute!" as if talking to Ada, less concerned about her boyfriend than the stupidity of dropping out of school.

But Alice took it in a different way, looking off toward one of Father's paintings but I am sure not seeing it, then after a minute saying,

"I'm flying to Paris," quietly but with some of the decisiveness of her years-ago *"Buy* the plane!" to me gasping at the cost of flying to Lexington.

I said, "Honey, you can't fly to Paris, with that leg!" and she kicked at the walking stick with her good leg, was silent for a minute then said, *"You* can. And I think you should. She's just a kid, you know."

I thought, Some kid! With a trust fund in a Lexington bank from her grandmother!—But I said (a one-step-at-a-time man), "First of all let's get her on the phone, see how she sounds" (her letters were far between, and seemed to be getting farther), and I dug up Madame Levrile's address which we used in writing her and after exasperating delays and exasperating accents managed to get Celeste's number—in French-English that I translated, hopefully, into figures.

Then hanging up as I noticed our clock; I said, It was after midnight over there, we'd better wait until morning, Alice kicking the walking stick again and murmuring, "More likely she'll be there," then, as if I was wasting time, "Call her!"

But she wasn't; far from it!—A difficult conversation, my French having suffered with the years and Celeste's English no better than before (to her ears a second-class language that no Parisians but taxi drivers had any need of); but after repeats back and forth as to who I was, whom I was trying to reach, it added up to: Mad'moiselle Embry had moved out months ago—"I beg your pardon?" "Pas de quoi, m'sieu"—no forwarding address, stopped in now and then for mail. "Phone" "Pas de phone, m'sieu. Peut-etre private nombere?"

A long moment of transatlantic silence while I tried to think I had misinterpreted the language but knew I hadn't, then a tangled linguistic request that mad'moiselle please ask Miss Embry to call home the next time she stopped in for mail. "Oui, mais oui, m'sieu. Etendu," and, "Merci, mad'moiselle," and in firm English from Alice in her chair with her leg straight out, "I know where she is!"

I said, "Maybe not," the same explanation already stumbling through my head. "And even so what can we—"

She said, "Who publishes this man's books? Ask the Library."

But when the Library gave me the publisher and I phoned him an annoyed young woman told me that communication with Bruce Renlap should be directed to the publisher who would forward appropriate material.

Something we should do, but what?—the days of indecision adding up. Suppose I went to Paris, or both of us went, what then? Board at Levrile's until she happened by for her mail? It might be weeks. And what would we see when she appeared? Surprise? Dismay? Resentment? Some indication, anyway, of the space between us now, her age and ours, her hopes and ours; of the desert of incomprehensions between twenty and sixty? And we there in a Paris as remote from the one we remembered as our longed-for child from the one we had imagined—

Then a ring of the phone one afternoon and, "Will you accept a collect call from Paris, France?", I saying, "Yes, of course," signaling for Alice on the sofa to lower the TV (my hearing going the way of Father's); two or three voices came through in French, then Ada's voice strong and cheerful: "Mummy? Dad?"— it used to me "Mama" and "Papa".

I said, "Hold on a second, honey, while I get your mother on the other phone," waving at Alice and laying it down to go to the phone in the kitchen. The first thing I heard on the kitchen phone was Alice's, "Married did you say!"

Then, "Yes, darling. I'm Mrs. Bruce G. Renlap. Isn't it wonderful! Bruce wants to speak to you. The call went through so fast he's in the midst of doing his famous omelette aux fines herbes but will be here—"

"You are married, honey?"

"Not only that, Mummy; I'm seven months along, and a sight—" Alice either dropping the phone or hanging up, I listening long enough to get an address and phone number.

Long enough to leave me standing at a window and seeing the call as a flight back across the generations, out of ours and into our child's and its up-to-date levels of beliefs and disbeliefs we were not prepared for—any more than we had been for the black mountain that once changed our course. . . .

We had to go to Atlanta to get a plane for France, everybody very helpful, considerate, offering a wheelchair (which she disdained), standing aside not to crowd her on the boarding stairs; she mounting slowly with the stick, step by step, hop by hop, and halfway up losing the stick, stumbling against me and before I could steady her, falling ten steps to the ground and lying there stunned and still, then beginning to whimper; the airport people much better prepared for such a thing than I was, covering her with a blanket, lifting her on to a stretcher that appeared out of nowhere, and then into an ambulance, a chubby young woman with a label on her shirt handing me the stick and pointing at the bench inside by the stretcher.

Painful, the hurt of it coming through to me in her squeezed-together eyelids, in the gripping of her fingers in mine, the right-left-right turns of her head on the pillow, all of it taking me back to the lightning flash at the Park (and my superstitious feeling of witnessing a change in our good luck).

But not as serious as it seemed: something twisted, strained, pulled, what not? but the X rays showed the old break intact. Cheerful young doctors decreasing day by day and indicating imminent dismissal; an afternoon visit from a bearded youth in white we hadn't seen before, very casual, very easy, sitting across from her chair after suggesting with a tilt of his head at the door that I leave them; then talking to me later in the hall, continuing his psychiatric palpations for hints as to why she had fallen at just that moment: Acrophobia? Reluctant to leave? Distasteful mission? (to all of

149

which I shook my head, though he may have been sharp enough to see I might have said more about "distasteful mission"). Then, from another white jacket, "Home tomorrow, Mrs. Embry. Four months and you'll be on the golf course," stirring her to a wan unbelieving smile.

Home, but with a change in herself, in her total being, as if her falls had disordered obscure adjustments—that maybe the nosy young man (psychiatrist, psychologist, whatever he was) had been searching for. Slow to recover; recovering physically from the fall but as if something else had been disjoined, some circuit that the fall (falls?) had shaken apart: dialing wrong phone numbers, striking wrong keys on her portable, writing—almost illegibly—wrong figures on checks, reading and re-reading the same page of a book. "Mustn't drive," from three doctors, to both of us; and later to me from one of them, "Nothing to be done," in a kindly voice; "My mother became the same way."

Very quiet when people from the School stopped by; nodding a weak thank-you to Jessica and the Doctor for the Indian-made silver brooch they brought her from Ecuador; refusing to talk to Sister Mary on the phone from Lexington: "You talk to her. Say I've gone out. Say I'm in the bathroom. Say I've got diarrhea."

Our talk was brief (not her favorite in-law, as I think I've mentioned), I telling her Alice had been a little under the weather lately but it was nothing serious; she asking about "little Ada and her boyfriend"—which I side-stepped with generalities—and ending with the announcement that Denis (their brother) might stop by on his way to Australia, "Horses again,"—rather bad news, considering everything, but I said, "Fine!" (as you have to do).

My mind turning at once as we ended our talk, to thinking, if he came, I would not mention to him the little moment with Alice in the kitchen though it was still on my mind, and troubled me out of all proportion to its significance (if it had any): Alice working at opening a can of something with a ten-inch carving knife, and I saying, "Try a can opener, honey." She turning on me, suddenly furious, knife at my belt buckle; then flinging it into the sink and stumbling out in tears.

And not mentioning it to Ada when she phoned one afternoon as I came in with a briefcase of papers to be graded; phoned from the hospital, "Just to say everybody's fine. . . .

151

A boy, eight-and-a-quarter pounds, everything in place. . . . 'Bruce, Junior.' Senior recovering nicely with the help of a fifth of Dom
Perignon. . . . How's Mummy?" I saying her
mother wasn't feeling so well today, but
nothing serious; wasn't "convenient to the
phone" (wondering if the little Southernism
would remind her of home). I said I would
pass on the good news—"good news."

Denis stoped by for half a day between
planes; must have been over the Pacific on the
morning I tried to wake my wife of thirty-two
years and found myself looking down at her
white-as-the-pillow face but hardly seeing it
for the feeling of solitude rising in my chest,
for the sudden tears in my eyes for myself and
the prospect of an Alice-less house, an Alice-
less life, more concerned with the disaster for
me of not having her than of her own not-
being.

Really not surprised at Ada's remoteness
when I called her—out of touch with home
and us for so long, such distance in years between us to begin with, and no doubt sensing
our antique prejudices about her marriage, her
life: "Dear me! Poor Dad!" half to herself, as if
my call had caught her at a bad moment; "And
no way I can leave to help you, baby sick,

husband grumpy," going on in a tight voice as if gathering up parcels she had dropped as she came in the door, something about "staged a nice splash before the South Africa embassy." Two or three arrests, Bruce among them; "pushed me off when I tried to join them, said I hadn't been trained for arrest. Can you tie that! They didn't hold him. And now he's talking about going to Mozambique." She wasn't going to Mozambique! Everything up in the air! "Sorry about Mummy, Dad. Chin up!— Both of us."

Winter by then and I turning at last to the odds and ends in Alice's desk and finding the note that was more to herself than to me, almost illegible, part of it in ink, part in pencil (suggesting interruptions, pauses, fadings):

But why is he coming so far, so out of his way, dear brother, who hasn't laid eyes on little sister for so many years and fears? Just passing through, they say (to confuse her—already confused enough); just stopping off on his way to—some place that didn't put her on his way at all, Hawaii, Formosa, somewhere out there, blue water, blue skies, blue islands away.

She knew why he was coming! He was coming to say good-by to little sister without seeming to say it, to see little sister once more before she became someone else.

The someone else she had already become, years, tears, fears ago, disguised now, masked as another, renamed by the turning-away doctors, one of those beautiful hospital names, Amentia, Leukemia, Sarcoma, all fit for a queen. Hard to think sometimes, as you feel for a door key with cold fingers, hard to finger up a needle, sew one thought to another. And resenting it, resentment held back, out of sight in a scrap-bag bursting with resentments—for being guided at doorways, at chairs, handed up and down trivial steps, at having to hear, "No more driving," from a son of a bitch in a white coat, breaking off her arms like the woman in the Louvre.

And HE—what's his name?—the still a stranger she married in another life—


Laying it down as the hard-to-read (hard-to-believe) writing seemed to link with the hard-to-believe "still-a-stranger" she had married, and perhaps with the one I had married—taking off my glasses as if expecting to see it better from a distance, and seeing first of all Sister Mary and her long-ago verdict of "You two" and the rest of it, and thinking today she might well add, "What did I tell you!" as vindicated by Sister Alice herself; and wondering as

154

I returned to my glasses if the sisters had talked of it between them, if the "not right for each other" had been a whispered judgment of both of them—

> . . . telling her in the kitchen, "Try a can opener, it's a can," as if she couldn't see straight, had lost her mind, she turning on him, knife in her fist, then knife into the sink like a forte with symbals.—Making up tales to confuse her, while he Waited with a capital W. And What's-her-name waited, the bitch, both of them handing her by the elbow up and down paltry bastard curbstones as if she'd lost her mind and couldn't—

And a few lines more that I would have read if the phone hadn't mercifully rung: "Will you accept a collect call from Bordeaux, France?" Bordeaux! but, "Yes, I will." "Go ahead, Bordeaux," as if with a nod over her shoulder, and, "Hello, Dad. Ada here."—Troubles again! More of the same: the bastard had moved out; two weeks ago, maybe three, maybe four, gone to Africa, Mozambique or some such place, she didn't know or care; had filed for divorce, was getting out of this fucking country the minute her papers went through, was on a short visit to a friend at Libourne, she and little Asa, while she got herself together—

*Berry Fleming*

"Little Who?"

"Little Asa, Dad. His middle name. I'm
dropping the 'Bruce' part." Would write in a
day or two, was phoning in case he called the
Paris number. "Will explain everything when I
see you. Can't think straight today, nowadays."

"When you see me?"

She was planning to join a college friend in
California, Santa Ynez; they would stop in on
their way, if that was convenient.—And, as if
noticing an unfastened button, "How are you,
darling? Is Ora Mae still with you? She can
help with Asa.—It *is* convenient, Dad? Just for
a week or so."

"Er, of course, honey"; what else could I say,
except to have skipped the "er"? (an old-style
father from the days of "Mama" and "Papa",
unable to explain, across the miles and the
years, that my daughter appearing with my
black grandson—even though it allowed me to
participate in my country's Tomorrow—created some problems between me and my
friends, me and my colleagues at the School, to
say nothing of between me and my black cook-
housekeeper). I did explain, though I'm not
sure she heard me, gave no sign of it, that I was
planning to move also, the house too much for
one.

156

·She back to herself with, "I'll let you know, Dad, keep you posted. Can't say how fast these things go through over here. . . ."

And nothing more from her for weeks on end, I turning back to closer quandries of my own—my old-style clocks ticking on indifferently toward winter: Should I move my life to simpler quarters? Should I offer to retire before my School Board politely nudged me? Should I turn my thinking to my old friend's delighted summary of his new bride?—"Not only a superior driver and an excellent cook, Allen, but a registered nurse." Did I want an old man's marriage; not for love, not for lust but for a presence, a voice, a reflecting comprehension? Where would you find such a bride short of a rainbow's end?—My clocks ticking on to winter; and on beyond to, "A sad tale's best for winter," in a sedated mumble from the Doctor half way to the hospital in the car with us, and, "I'll tell it softly, Millie, yond' crickets shall not hear it," and Millie leaning over to lay a hand on his shoulder.

I turning back to my snapshots, my discards, flaring in the fireplace, sorry for a moment I had burned the one of my friends on the steps, Millie in a corner of the picture, in a swing on the porch; twenty-one at her birthday party— making her what today? Forty-six?

But where? (if I should be fool enough to want to hear her voice). The housekeeper at the Fort might know; Aunt Something-or-other—Aunt Vertice!

And a short back-and-forth on a call to the Officers Quarters that, hanging up, I thought had much in common with my burning of out-of-date snapshots: "Miss Vertice, please," (I couldn't remember the rest of her name, if I had ever heard it). "Who!" "Miss Vertice, the housekeeper." "Hold on. Wait a minute. Here's the housekeeper."

"Yes? Can I help you?" "Miss Vertice? Is this Miss Vertice?" "Miss Vertice is no longer with us. This is Mrs. Warren; can I help you?" (giving me a sense of swallowing a time-capsule, gagging a little).

"I need to get a phone number from Miss Vertice; can you tell me how to reach her, please?" "Miss Vertice retired in 1979" (another capsule to swallow); "Who is this calling, please?"

"My name is Embry, Allen Embry. I used to know Miss Vertice. I'd like to get a phone number from her." "I am sorry, Mr. Umber, but Miss Vertice died two years ago on a cruise to Hawaii."

"Oh!—Well, I'm sorry to hear that" (sorry

indeed!—for the tie to my search, the end of one, the end of both). "I'm really trying to get in touch with Miss Vertice's niece." "I'm Aunt Vertice's niece, Mr. Umber; one of them. I'm Millie."

A short blackout while I fumbled with that—and with the "Mr. Umber"—then something like, "You are Millie, my God! Your voice—"

"I don't understand, Mr. Umber—"

"And you are now Mrs. Warren, Millie?"

"I am sorry, Mr. Umber, but I am very busy—"

"Thank you, Mrs. Warren," and hanging up quickly before I heard any more. . . .

When were the movers coming? Yes, Thursday. "Thursday at eight-fifteen, Mr. Embry?"/ Mr. Umber. "Yes. All right."